Knave
of
Hearts

Books by Jasmine Cresswell

Knave of Hearts
For Love of Christy
One Step to Paradise
Master Touch
Dear Adam
Under Cover of Night
Surprised by Love
Refuge in His Arms
Imprisoned Heart
Tender Triumph
Runaway Love
Stormy Reunion

Knave
of
Hearts

Jasmine Cresswell

SPEAKING VOLUMES, LLC

NAPLES, FLORIDA

2012

Knave of Hearts

ISBN 978-1-61232-811-9

Chapter One

THE BACKYARD BIRTHDAY party for little Tod Weaver had been going on too long. Linda could see that her twins were getting dangerously bored. They had already watered the flowers with soda pop and mashed their servings of chocolate cake into a gooey mess on their paper plates. Drew was temporarily content to sit and suck his sticky fingers, but Kate's eyes had acquired a speculative gleam that Linda recognized all too well. Definitely time to go home, she decided. The twins had reached the limits of their good behavior. Any second now, Kate would realize the intriguing possibilities of chocolate cake when used as finger paint. She would point out these possibilities to her brother, and soon no surface would be safe from their joint attack.

Ignoring their howls of protest, Linda grabbed each child by an elbow—one of the few places free of chocolate—and dragged them off to be washed under the garden hose. Kate, of course, stuck her head straight into the cold spray, then chuckled with delight as she peered up at her mother through a curtain of wet brown curls.

"More!" she demanded with three-year-old arrogance. "More water, Mommy! Make Drew wet, too."

Becky Weaver, Tod's mother, laughed as she walked by. "Not much like you, are they, Lindy Beth? I bet you

1

never got so much as a crumb of birthday cake on your clothes."

Linda smiled. "No, I guess I didn't."

"You were everybody's little Miss Perfect." Becky grinned. "Lord, how I hated it when my mother kept telling me how wonderful you were. For me, the high point of second grade was the day Matt Deighton cornered you in the playground and poured red paint over your new skirt. Do you remember?"

"Matt was always doing something outrageous," Linda said, avoiding a direct answer. "I was just quiet and studied hard." She pulled a handkerchief from the pocket of her tailored beige bermudas and wiped the twins' damp fingers. "I was a long way from being perfect."

Becky stared at the pristine hanky, then blew upward to lift a limp strand of hair from her forehead. "Lindy Beth, you're *still* perfect," she said with a trace of envy. "Good grief, I bet there isn't another woman in town who carries a starched and ironed linen handkerchief."

Linda kept her smile carefully in place. "Nobody else has twins. I've learned to be prepared."

"But look at you!" Becky wailed. "Two hours at a backyard party for preschoolers, and your clothes aren't even mussed. How in the world do you do it?"

"My mother's training, I guess. You know what a perfectionist she is."

"I sure do. She'd have driven me crazy in five minutes. I don't know how you made it through high school without rebelling."

Linda concentrated on wiping a blob of chocolate from Drew's ear. "I wasn't quite the paragon everybody thought," she murmured.

Becky chuckled. "Honey, making straight A's, then

taking a degree in domestic science and marrying the local minister isn't exactly kicking over the traces. You and Jim were a storybook couple." Her smile faded, and she looked anxiously at Linda. "I'm sorry. I didn't mean to put my foot in my mouth again."

"You didn't, Becky." Linda tried to sound genuinely reassuring. In the nearly three years since Jim's death, the townspeople of Carson had tried so hard to protect her from the pain of his loss that their efforts had long since become more burdensome than her actual widowhood. She was relieved when a bellow of rage from Tod caught Becky's attention, breaking the awkward silence.

Becky wrinkled her nose. "Uh-oh! Sounds like my little birthday boy is working up to a major tantrum. He reminds me of my mother-in-law when he yells like that. Catch you later, Lindy Beth!"

"Yes, and thanks for inviting us over today. We had a great time."

"Fank you," Kate intoned solemnly, imitating her mother. She smiled through her tangled hair with the sublime confidence of a child who knows she is well loved. "Bye-bye, Tod's mommy." She nudged Drew. "Say fank you to Tod's mommy."

Drew remained stubbornly silent, and Becky shrugged, tousling his hair. "Still a man of few words, huh, Drew?" Another shriek from her own son set her running. "Thanks for coming, kids, and thanks for Tod's birthday present."

The twins were tired enough to be unusually cooperative as they walked down the hot street toward home, and Linda didn't attempt to start a conversation. She was angry, she realized with a jolt of surprise—angry to the point where her heart pounded and her breath came in small, uneven gasps. And the strangest thing was, she didn't understand what was bothering her. Surely she wasn't allowing herself to get worked up over Becky Weaver's casual remarks? Heaven knew, by now she ought to be used to the way the townsfolk regarded her. Carson, Colorado, like most other small towns, had a way of fitting its citizens into slots and then making sure that people stayed where they'd been put.

Linda knew exactly where she stood in Carson's scheme of things. Her niche had been determined from the day she was adopted by Nora and Ron Owen. Her adoptive parents had enjoyed a long reign as pillars of the church and the town's most upright citizens. When they adopted a baby daughter after fourteen years of childless marriage, the blue-eyed, golden-haired girl was immediately declared "a little angel" and "a gift from heaven." Having given this "angel" their stamp of approval, the townsfolk made no secret of the fact that they expected Lindy Beth to live up to the role she had been assigned. Subtly, in a thousand different ways, they reminded her how fortunate she was to have been adopted into such a wonderful family.

Linda obediently struggled to be the perfect child her parents and everybody else wanted. While other toddlers splashed through dirt puddles and crushed Play-Doh into the carpet, she sat quietly and looked at her picture books. She never stuck her fingers into an electrical outlet to find out what was behind the wall socket. She never drank laundry detergent because it was a pretty shade of blue. She remembered to brush her teeth without being told, and always went to bed the first time she was asked.

Sally Deighton, who lived next door to the Owens, was virtually the only person in Carson to protest Lindy Beth's rigid upbringing.

"Poor little tyke," she remarked one day when she came over to take coffee with Nora. Sally's eyes softened with pity as she watched Lindy Beth nibble at a plain cracker, her frilly dress covered by a paper napkin. "You're protecting that poor child to death, Nora. Mark my words, she'll explode one day from sheer frustration."

Nora Owen treated this prediction with contempt. She had a low opinion of Sally, and Linda frequently heard Nora elaborate on the subject. Sally Deighton considered herself an artist, and she occupied a low notch on the totem pole of Carson townswomen. Everybody knew she spent far too much time in her garage messing around with lumps of clay when she should have been tidying her house. Her husband often had to cook his own meals, and her children were left to run wild, which had already proven disastrous as far as Matt, her oldest son, was concerned. The oldest Deighton boy had been an impossible toddler and a thorn in the side of his teachers from the day he started school. The Owens were sure Sally Deighton knew nothing about raising a precious, adorable child like Lindy Beth.

Linda knew her mother had never been able to understand why her dear little Lindy Beth had chosen one of the wild Deighton children as her very best friend. She reproached her daughter constantly, but on this one subject Lindy Beth couldn't be persuaded to change her mind. She and Jennifer Deighton were inseparable from the moment they first met in the Deighton sandbox, and they stayed best friends right through high school. The Owens were very relieved when Jennifer won a scholarship to the School of Journalism at Columbia University.

"New York's just the place for a young woman like her," Nora remarked grimly. "It's all actresses and models living there, and none of them any better than they ought to be."

Lindy Beth won a scholarship, too. She was awarded a grant to study at the Art Institute in Philadelphia. Her parents didn't worry—at least not much. They knew—surely they could count on it?—that Lindy Beth was too well behaved to accept a scholarship to art school.

Linda listened as her father boasted nervously to his cronies that *his* daughter had more sense than to waste her time messing around with a bunch of East Coast artists and weirdos. The men of Carson nodded their heads approvingly. Pretty girls had no need to take themselves off to distant colleges when they could find plenty of local boys willing to marry them. Women only stuffed their heads full of damfool education when they were afraid of being left on the shelf.

Naturally, the Owens didn't believe a word of it when Sally Deighton marched over to inform them that Lindy Beth had cried herself to sleep for three weeks straight after sending her letter of refusal to the Art Institute.

"Huh!" Nora commented as soon as Sally was out of earshot. "Did you hear what that woman just said, Lindy Beth? What rubbish! You don't want to go away to college, do you?" Without pausing for breath she rushed into her next sentence. "Sally Deighton doesn't understand a *thing* about raising children. She should do something about that dreadful son of hers instead of worrying about our dear little girl, and I'll tell her so next time she comes sticking her nose into our business. There's no discipline in her house, that's the problem."

For a while that summer, even though the scholarship had been safely refused, Linda gave the Owens cause to fear that she might actually rebel. Their previously angelic daughter stayed out till all hours, refusing to say where she'd been. Once she had even barricaded herself in the bedroom behind a chest of drawers saying that she wanted peace and quiet to work on a painting. "A painting, for heaven's sake!" Nora protested.

Then, like a welcome thunderstorm after a period of increasing tension, the scandal over Matt Deighton and Suzanne Mackenzie broke. Nora Owen thanked her lucky stars when she saw that dear little Lindy Beth's common sense returned as soon as the dreadful truth about Matt Deighton was revealed. Matt left town, narrowly avoiding arrest. A week later, Lindy Beth agreed to attend college in Grand Junction. She even promised to return home every weekend "to save money," and by attending summer classes, to graduate in three years.

From the moment Matt left town, Lindy Beth returned to her old, delightful self. The Owens were jubilant when their daughter started dating Jim Petrie, the assistant minister at Carson's Community Church.

Lindy Beth announced her engagement to Jim Petrie after morning service on Easter Sunday. For once, even Sally Deighton had nothing outrageous to say. She congratulated Jim on his good taste and kissed Linda soundly. Then, as soon as she could, she hurried over to confer with her husband, who was stacking Bibles at the rear of the church. She would have been horrified to realize that Linda had also returned to the church in search of her mother's new leather gloves, and was kneeling down between the pews, not ten yards away.

"The town organized this engagement," Sally remarked sadly to her husband. "They decided Carson's resident angel would make the perfect wife for a minister, and they threw the two of them together."

"I'm surprised her parents didn't break things up."

"Why would they? They're smart enough to see this

marriage is the closest they'll ever get to keeping the poor kid at home forever."

"She should have gone away to college," Frank Deighton commented. "The Owens don't see what a high price she pays for living out their fantasies." His wife was silent, and he added, "Do you think Jim Petrie really loves her?"

"Sure. Why shouldn't he? Everybody loves Lindy Beth. She works her tail off at being lovable."

"But does *she* love *him?*"

"How would she know? The average eighth-grader knows more about love than Linda."

There was silence. Linda peeked over the top of the pew and watched Frank Deighton, who seemed very occupied with Bible-stacking.

"Are you sure she's so innocent?" he asked finally. "What about that summer before Matt left home? It's hard to see your kids objectively, but I'd have thought our son was a powerful teacher where love and sex are concerned."

"Who knows what really happened that summer? Matt never told anybody, and I'm darn sure Linda didn't tell the truth."

"You can't blame her for that. She was too naive to understand how important her testimony was. And all that pressure from her parents would have been too much for anybody. It's not surprising she decided it was better to let everybody think Matt had spent all those long summer nights with the Mackenzie girl."

Sally Deighton ran her hands impatiently through her short-cropped hair. "Of course I understood the pressure her parents applied. I just hoped she might be clear-sighted enough to see that Matt wouldn't have done what Coach Mackenzie accused him of."

"Unfortunately, the coach and his daughter told a pretty convincing story."

"I guess they did. Anyway, that's all water under the bridge now. I'm sure Matt never gives Linda a second thought these days. He seems to have a more exciting woman in tow each time he calls."

"So why all the fuss about Lindy's engagement?"

"Darn it all, Frank, the poor girl's never had the freedom to sneeze without somebody handing her a tissue, and now she'll be trussed up tighter than she was before. She has too much potential to throw it all away before she even realizes what she's missing."

"I guess you can't make a person live up to their potential if they don't want to. It's not like the old days, when you encouraged her to stick her fingers in the cookie batter and mess up her clothes."

"She'll never be really happy with Jim Petrie."

"How can you be so sure? She's become the person everybody wants her to be. She'll probably have a wonderful life with the minister. After all, he seems like a genuinely nice guy."

"Linda doesn't need to marry a nice guy. She ought to marry somebody who'll encourage her to rebel. She has talent, Frank. Real artistic talent that shouldn't go to waste."

Frank Deighton grinned. "Sally, love, it's time to face facts. Be satisfied that our three kids are all out there in the big world, doing their own thing. Accept that Lindy Beth Owen is destined to remain a virtuous pillar of the local community."

The wedding date was fixed for one week after Lindy Beth's graduation from college, and Jennifer came home from New York to act as maid of honor. The townsfolk were disappointed to find that she looked attractive—and not at all ruined—in an elegant burgundy satin gown.

Lindy Beth, however, was the unquestioned star of the day. Nora Owen wept tears of pride as her daughter floated down the aisle looking ravishing in clouds of filmy white nylon lace. Matt Deighton had the decency to stay away and his parents were kind enough not to suggest to anyone that Lindy Beth's virginal white might not be entirely justified.

The wedding reception went off without a hitch, and the newlyweds left for their two-week honeymoon in San Francisco. With the magic efficiency expected of her, Lindy Beth returned home to Carson already pregnant. By this time, she was so good at disguising her true feelings that nobody suspected this immediate plunge into parenthood left Linda feeling scared and inadequate.

The twins—a boy and a girl—were born punctually nine months later, in March. The proud grandparents and the townsfolk in general declared them adorable. A shower was organized for the new babies and, Carson congratulated itself on the certainty that Lindy Beth and Jim Petrie were destined to grow old and gray together—Carson's own smiling answer to Darby and Joan.

The optimistic predictions proved premature. Even now, close to three years after the accident, people still had a hard time expressing their feelings about the unseasonably cold night in September when Jim Petrie had been driving home from a pastoral visit to old Mrs. Hanneker.

According to the story pieced together afterward, the minister had seen smoke coming from the windows of the Johnson house. He immediately stopped his car, ran up to the front porch, pounded on the door, and alerted the family. In all the confusion that ensued in evacuating the house and calling the fire department from a neighbor's telephone, nobody noticed when little Shaun Johnson ran back inside the house, intent upon rescuing his kitten from a back bedroom. When his frantic mother finally realized her youngest child was missing, the Johnson home was already an inferno of heat and leaping flames. Jim had run into the burning house without a thought for his personal safety. To the eternal gratitude of the Johnsons, he managed to save their son. The tragedy for the town was that their brave young minister died of his burns.

And so, very suddenly, Linda found herself a widow. Her heart-shaped face took on a new and more ethereal beauty as grief hollowed her cheekbones and bruised her eyes with shadows. Her slenderness threatened to become gauntness.

The town of Carson watched her suffering with dismay, and did their best to alleviate it. The mayor led a drive to establish a memorial trust fund for the twins, and the church congregation would have been willing to wait several months before appointing a new assistant minister just so they wouldn't need to turn poor Lindy Beth out of her church-owned house. Fortunately, Mr. and Mrs. Owen solved the problem of where Lindy Beth and the twins would live. Their daughter's place was back home with them, they said firmly, and Linda, numbed by grief and overwhelmed by the unrelenting demands of the twins, consented with scarcely a murmur.

At twenty-two, Linda was once again living in her parents' home. If it hadn't been for the twins, people might almost have forgotten she had ever left.

· Linda felt Kate tug at her bermudas. "We're here," Kate said. "Where's Grandad?"

"Inside with Granny, I guess." Linda slammed a mental door shut on her string of memories. She unlatched the gate, and the twins hurtled across the front yard. At least they were pleased to be home, Linda thought, then wondered why she could hardly bring herself to turn into the gate.

Her reluctance to enter the house was ridiculous, and she gave her shoulders a brisk shake. She sprinted to catch up with the twins. "Come on, kids," she said, swinging them up the shallow steps to the front door. "Gosh, you're both filthy. You'd better have your baths early tonight."

She unlocked the door, and they all trooped into the immaculate kitchen. The counters gleamed with their usual white brilliance, and the familiar smell of pine disinfectant tickled Linda's nose. She smiled wryly. If the people of Carson ever held a contest for the most germ-free environment, her mother's kitchen would win hands down.

She heard two pairs of footsteps hurrying down the narrow hallway. "Lindy Beth! Is that you? Are you home?"

"Yes, Mother, we're home."

Nora and Ron Owen arrived in the kitchen together. "Grandad! I had choklec cake!" Drew tore across the room and launched himself into his grandfather's arms.

Ron's eyes twinkled. "I can see you did, young man."

Kate leaned against his knee. "We had soda pop, too. And chips."

Nora Owen clicked her tongue. "They'll probably be up all night, sick to their stomachs."

Linda and her father exchanged glances. "I'll take these two upstairs and give them a bath," Ron said. He nodded to his daughter, and she wondered if she was imagining the worry in his expression. "Talk to you later, Lindy Beth, when these little monsters are in bed."

The twins skipped out of the kitchen, clutching their grandfather's hands, and Linda walked across to the sink. "Want some tea, Mom?"

"No, not right now, thanks." Nora compressed her lips in irritation. "There's a smudge of dirt on your leg, dear—you'd better wipe it off. You can't expect the twins to keep neat and tidy if their own mother goes around with dirt on her knees."

Linda obediently dampened a paper towel and cleaned the almost-invisible smear of dust from her knee. She waited in silence for the rest of the inevitable lecture. For once, however, her mother didn't seem interested in pursuing the theme of cleanliness being next to Godliness. She seemed, in fact, to be bursting with impatience to impart some news.

"Lindy Beth, I'm afraid this is going to come as a horrible shock to you. You'll never guess who Mrs. Wittmeyer saw driving through town last night."

Linda smiled. "No, Mom, I'm sure I wouldn't. Is Bert Hayden home for the summer? Or maybe the mayor. Did the mayor finally ask Rita Lindstrop for a date?"

"It's no laughing matter, Lindy Beth, as you'll soon find out. Mrs. Wittmeyer saw *Jennifer Deighton* driving along Main Street on her way home from the airport in Grand Junction." Nora Owen paused for dramatic effect. "And she had her brother with her."

Linda's laughter faded, and was replaced by an expression of careful blankness. "You mean Brian Deighton's come home with Jennifer?" she asked. "But I thought he was in Germany with the air force."

"Of course I don't mean Brian! I mean her older

brother, that dreadful Matthew! According to Mrs. Wittmeyer, he looks as disreputable as ever. Still needs a haircut, and she says he's probably wearing the same pair of jeans he left home in. The man obviously doesn't have a penny to bless himself with."

Linda's stomach performed a high-flying backflip into her shoes. After seven years, and all that had happened in between, she was astonished that hearing Matt's name could still have such an impact on her emotions. Fortunately, she'd managed to learn a few survival skills in the last few years. As a child, she had coped with the burden of too much parental love by behaving perfectly. Now she coped with the same parental demands by keeping every trace of genuine emotion hidden, except from the twins. With the ease of long practice, she stretched her mouth into a fair imitation of a casual smile.

"The Deightons will be glad to see their son at home after all this time," she said. "They've visited him in New York, of course, but Sally says Matt's been up to his eyebrows in work these past couple years."

"Huh! You notice she never says exactly what this mysterious work that he's been doing *is*. Sally Deighton never would hear a word said against that boy, even when everybody warned her what sort of character he was. Up to his eyebrows in work, indeed. Up to his eyebrows in *jail*, more likely."

Linda felt an unexpected flare of white-hot anger on Matt's behalf, but she didn't say anything. She'd spent most of her twenty-five years not saying things that might hurt or offend her parents, and by now suppressing her anger was automatic, something she rarely needed to think about.

"I forgot. Did you say if you wanted some tea?" she

asked, fighting to control the rage still shivering through her.

"I may as well, I guess. But I can make it. You sit down and take it easy till Kate and Drew come down for supper. Those two would exhaust anybody. They're not a bit like you used to be at their age."

Thank God, Linda reflected silently.

Nora put on the kettle and reached for the box of tea bags. "Now, Lindy Beth, I know I can count on you to be sensible about this. You're not going to see that dreadful Matthew while he's in town, are you?"

"He probably won't be here for long. I don't suppose any of us will see him."

"Mrs. Wittmeyer says he's home for two whole weeks."

Linda didn't ask how Mrs. Wittmeyer knew Matthew Deighton's personal plans within twelve hours of his reaching town. With some justification, Mrs. Wittmeyer prided herself on having a complete and intimate knowledge of everybody else's business in the entire county of Carson, which made it all the more remarkable that she had never heard any whisper about Matt and Linda's relationship that long-ago summer.

Linda felt a curious, half-forgotten ache of longing squeeze tight around her lungs. Odd how only Matt— sinful, teasing, irresponsible Matt—had ever caused that quickening of her pulses, that ridiculous fluttering of her heart. If only Jim—dear, good, honest Jim—had ever provoked anything close to the same reaction, maybe their marriage would have had a chance.

Even the thought seemed disloyal, and Linda spoke quickly. "Kettle's boiling, Mom."

Her mother made the tea, continuing all the while to harp on the subject of Matt Deighton and his unwelcome return. A great believer in saying what she thought, it apparently never occurred to Nora that Linda often felt bludgeoned by her mother's passion for forthright speech. Linda sighed. Since her mother always believed that what she wanted was entirely for "Lindy Beth's good," there was no chance of persuading her to change the topic of conversation. Nora Owen would press on doggedly until Linda agreed with her. Usually, there didn't seem much point in resisting, since Linda knew she'd have to give way in the end.

Nora poured two cups of tea, not at all put out by her daughter's silence. "If that horrible man's going to be home for the next few weeks, you want to make it plain right from the start that you'll have nothing to do with him. You know he's trouble, Lindy Beth. Give that sort an inch, and he'll take a hundred miles. Look what happened that summer before you went to college. Of course, you were only eighteen and far too young to know what he was trying to do to you—"

"He was trying to get me to sleep with him," Linda said softly. "But don't worry, Mom. After seven years in New York, I imagine Matthew Deighton has more exciting plans for the summer than seducing the widow next door. Not every man in the world is trying to beat a path to my bed, you know."

Nora winced. Despite her much-vaunted delight in directness, there were several subjects—nearly all related to sex—that she preferred to approach by comfortable circumlocutions. Linda could almost see what her mother was thinking. Nora would be asking herself why "Little Lindy Beth" had recently begun to speak with such shocking frankness, and no doubt she was mentally blaming television or the movies. As far as Nora was concerned, TV programming had been on a downward moral curve ever since the cancellation of *I Love Lucy* and *Leave It to Beaver*.

Nora scoured out the teapot, scrubbed the counter, and returned everything to its appointed spot in the cupboards before sitting down to drink her cup of tea. "Lindy Beth, I'm warning you to watch out for that man. He's the next best thing to a rapist, so you can't be too careful. Remember, he not only ruined Suzanne Mackenzie, but he tried to take advantage of you once, and there's no saying but what he'd do it again. After all, you're a woman alone in the world, aren't you?"

Alone! Linda thought with a sudden tinge of hysteria. Dear God, if only she could be alone — really alone — for even a day! Or half a day, maybe. She quelled a hiccup of laughter, replying with her usual mildness, "Matt isn't a rapist, Mom. You know he was never even arrested, much less brought to trial and found guilty. What's more, there are a lot of people in Carson apart from me who know he didn't rape Suzanne Mackenzie. He always denied he was even with her that night, and he would never have forced her to have sex against her will."

Nora Owen gave this suggestion the contemptuous sniff it deserved. "How would you know? That boy was heading for trouble from the moment he got thrown out of school. Don't you go letting that soft heart of yours get the better of your common sense, Lindy Beth."

"It never has in the past," Linda said with unexpected self-mockery. "Somehow, I've always managed to take darned good care of myself. Whoever else gets into trouble, I always end up doing okay, with everybody in town telling me how wonderful I am."

Her mother looked at her sharply, but at that moment the kitchen doorbell rang and Linda jumped to her feet. "I'll get it," she said.

She pulled open the latch, then felt her fingers freeze around the handle. Matt Deighton stood on the doorstep, one hand raised to the bell, the other tucked casually in his pocket. His six feet two of solidly muscled body blocked out the brilliant sun, casting a shadow that stretched all the way into the kitchen. He wore faded jeans and a cotton T-shirt, but the nondescript clothes did nothing to mute the stunning effect of thick blond hair and dark blue eyes that danced with silent laughter in a tanned, rugged face. Matt's years of alleged wild living hadn't robbed him of one ounce of his fatal good looks. In fact, experience seemed to have added a dangerously attractive gloss of maturity and sophistication to what had been nothing more than a raw, untutored sexuality.

Linda drew in a quick, involuntary breath. Fortunately, Matt wasn't looking at her. His impudent grin widened as he tipped his fingers to his forehead in a mocking salute to her mother. "Hello, Mrs. Owen. How are you doing? You look well."

Nora recovered her poise with the swiftness that befitted a civic leader and pillar of the church. "I'm doing nicely, thank you, Matt. Sure is a surprise to see you here. We didn't expect you back in Carson any time soon."

"I decided it was time for me to come home." He glanced briefly toward Linda. "I have some unfinished business to take care of, and the time seems right." He leaned comfortably against the doorjamb, not seeming to notice that he hadn't been invited in.

"Coach Mackenzie's still at the high school," Nora said. "Suzanne left town, but I did hear tell her baby got put up for adoption."

"I didn't leave town because of the Mackenzies," Matt said. "I didn't come back because of them, either." He turned away without waiting for Nora's reply, and Linda saw a faint hardening at the edges of his smile. "I was sent over here with a message for you, Lindy Beth. My mother would like to invite you and the twins to join us for supper tomorrow night. Jennifer got called back to Denver today, or she'd have been over to visit before now, but she's flying into Grand Junction again in the morning."

"It's very kind of your mother," Linda said quickly, all too aware of her mother's anxious presence right behind her. "But I don't think—"

"Mom said to remind you that your parents will be bowling and there's no reason for you to eat alone. Besides, Jennifer won't take no for an answer." He smiled ironically. "That's one of the problems of living in a small town, Linda. Everybody knows how everybody else spends their nights. Makes polite excuses difficult to come by. If you don't want to come to dinner, you'll have to give a flat-out no."

From the waves of outrage rippling toward her, Linda could tell that her mother was about to burst the fragile dam of her self-control. She spoke quickly, surprising herself by her answer. "I'd love to bring the twins over for supper and see Jen again. As long as it's no trouble for your mom. Please thank her and say how much I'm looking forward to catching up on all of the family news. Could I bring dessert or something?"

Matt's smile caused an odd little chill to ripple down Linda's arms. "You do that so well," he said. "I could almost believe that you really wanted to come to dinner."

Linda swallowed hard, forcing herself to look up at him. It was harder to do than she would have believed possible. "I don't know what you're talking about, Matt. You know how much I've always enjoyed spending time with your family."

For a moment, his dark eyes locked with hers, then

he shrugged lightly. "Have you ever considered what it would feel like if you told yourself the truth?" he asked. "Not other people necessarily, but at least yourself. The truth can be amazingly liberating, you know."

She flushed with indignation, forgetting her mother's presence in the heat of the moment. "I *always* tell the truth, Matthew Deighton. Always."

His gaze swept over her, infuriatingly sympathetic. "Poor Lindy Beth," he murmured. "I think you really believe what you're saying. Maybe you always did. Have a good day, Mrs. Owen."

With a casual wave to her mother, he turned and strolled down the neatly swept garden path.

"Well!" Nora Owen exclaimed, a wealth of suppressed emotion contained in the single word. "Well, Lindy Beth, what did I tell you? That man's out to make trouble."

Chapter Two

MATT JOINED HIS family in the backyard just as Linda and the twins were getting ready to leave.

"Did you get the job?" Frank asked his son eagerly.

Matt shook his head. "They haven't reached a decision yet, Dad. I have to call back on Monday."

"I'm keeping my fingers crossed for you." Jennifer smiled up at her brother.

"Thanks, but it's no big deal if it falls through."

"What sort of a job are you hoping to get, Matt?" Linda asked politely. It had been such a relief to find him absent for most of the evening that she felt she could afford to be friendly now.

"Construction," he replied after a brief pause. He squatted down so that he was almost at eye-level with the twins. "We haven't met," he said to the children. "My name's Matt Deighton, and I knew your mom when she was just a little girl. What are your names?"

Kate looked at him thoughtfully. "He is Drew," she said finally. "Me is Kate." She held up three fingers, sticking them almost under Matt's nose. "We is both this many years old 'cos we is twins."

"Three is a pretty good age," Matt said. "Do you know when you and your brother will be four?"

"When it's our birthday." She pushed her hair out of

her eyes, looking scornful at the foolishness of his question.

Jennifer laughed softly. "Your fatal charm with women doesn't seem to be working tonight, Matt."

He grinned. "Nope, it sure isn't. Guess I'll have to drive into town and soothe my wounded pride with one of the big girls."

Sally Deighton looked up from her seat on the hammock. "Walk Linda home first, would you please, Matt? Drew's almost asleep on his feet, and Kate isn't all that wide awake."

Linda spoke quickly. "Oh, I can manage, Sally. There's no need to trouble Matt—"

"It's no trouble," Matt interjected, swinging Drew up into his arms. "Anyway, I wanted to talk to you about something, Linda, and now's as good a time as any."

The fence between the Deighton and the Owen houses had once contained a convenient child-sized gap for squeezing from one yard to another. Nowadays, visitors had to trek from front door to front door, which could seem a long journey with two half-sleeping children. Linda realized she would only appear foolish if she protested too much about accepting Matt's help. Besides, there was no logical reason for her to feel uncomfortable about being alone with him. She had behaved badly that long-ago summer, but she had been scarcely eighteen and too terrified to give Matt the support he deserved. In retrospect, she realized that his cold, scornful anger at their final meeting had been justified. But all those old wounds must have long since healed. The tension she felt vibrating between them was probably no more than a product of her overactive imagination.

Linda lifted the sleepy but still protesting Kate into her arms and made her thanks to the Deightons. "We'll

get together tomorrow morning," Jennifer promised.
"But not too early. I'm going to sleep in and make the
most of my vacation."

A chorus of cheerful, slightly somnolent good-byes
followed Linda's and Matt's progress out of the backyard. Linda reflected that her mother would by now
have been elbow-deep in soapsuds, but Sally Deighton
saw no particular virtue in washing up and had served
everything on paper plates. The few utensils that
couldn't be thrown away had been carried into the
kitchen and left to soak in the sink until somebody felt
energetic enough to wash them. Linda smiled as she
pictured her mother's horror at such lackadaisical house-
keeping.

Matt spoke softly over Drew's sleeping head. "I'll
trade my thoughts for yours. Yours look as if they might
be amusing."

Linda chuckled. "Not really. I was thinking about
washing up."

"A few years ago, I'd have asked you to explain
what was funny about greasy dishes, but nowadays I'm
too smart to ask. When I hit the ripe old age of twenty-
eight, I finally realized there are some higher areas of
the brain where men will never be able to follow
women."

"I detect a subtle hint of male chauvinism lurking
behind that remark."

Matt grinned. "Just because I suggested women
didn't have quite the same thought patterns as men?"

His smile had lost none of its old potency during his
exile in New York, and Linda's arms tightened involun-
tarily around her daughter. "Is we going home?" Kate
asked, jolted out of her half-sleep.

"Yes, we are," Linda replied as they walked out of

the Deightons' front yard onto the sidewalk. "It's way past your bedtime, Katie."

"No," Kate said. "Not bedtime."

Never one to be outdone when the opportunity presented itself for saying no, Drew opened his eyes just long enough to speak. "Not bedtime," he denied vehemently. "I not tired. I playing." His head collapsed back onto Matt's chest.

Matt looked down at the nearly sleeping child with obvious amusement. "A man of few words but strong convictions, I see."

"Very strong," Linda agreed with a rueful sigh. "It's of absolutely no interest to Kate and Drew that all the childcare manuals say toddlers outgrow their negative attitudes before their third birthday. As far as this pair is concerned, the terrible twos look like lasting till high school."

"Better teach them to read. Your kids can't expect you to do a decent job of parenting unless you're all studying the same books. Just make sure they don't reach the section on adolescence too soon."

She laughed. "It's a thought." She balanced Kate on her hip so that one of her hands was free, then pushed a stray curl out of her eyes. "You said you had something you wanted to ask me."

"Did I? Oh, yes. It was about the Rumbles."

She looked up at him, startled. "The Rumbles? Who told you about them?"

"My mother. She sent me a couple of drawings last month. She says you've done a whole series, and they're very good."

Linda blushed. "She's prejudiced."

"Yes, she is. That's why I want to look at the entire series myself, if you'll let me."

Linda smiled wryly. "You're supposed to insist that

my drawings are wonderful, not agree that your mother's prejudiced."

He shrugged. "If your work's important to you, you don't want to hear polite lies. My mother looks at your drawings with the eyes of love, and we both know that's likely to affect her judgment. She claims you've come up with a really original idea for a family of make-believe animals called the Rumbles, and that you've drawn up some excellent patterns for making a series of soft toys. Usually, I'd trust her opinion without question. But she thinks of you as almost family, so I need to take a long, hard look for myself."

Linda forced herself to speak matter-of-factly, although she always found it difficult to discuss her work. "I don't know how original my concept is, but I'm fairly sure the patterns are commercially viable."

"Do you have enough professional training to back up that judgment?"

"I think so. I took several excellent courses in commercial art and fashion design when I was at college. It wasn't too difficult to adapt those techniques to what I was trying to do with the Rumbles."

"Could I see the drawings, Linda?"

She leaned against her parents' front door, glad of the familiar burden of Kate's body weighing down her arms. She felt oddly vulnerable at the prospect of exposing the Rumbles to Matt's inspection. Even if he hadn't managed to make it in New York as a professional artist, he had formidable natural talent. He would know at once if her drawings had any real promise. She didn't look at him when she spoke.

"I haven't shown the Rumbles to anybody except your mother. Why do you want to see them, Matt?"

He hesitated for a moment. "Because I happen to have a friend who's the president of the Playbrite toy company. I'm not promising anything, but if the patterns live up to my mother's claims, I might be able to interest his company in producing your Rumbles collection commercially."

Linda straightened abruptly, causing Kate to make a sleepy protest. To achieve commercial success with the Rumbles had been her secret fantasy for months. But now that Matt was actually offering her the chance to test her fantasy in the harsh light of day, she wasn't sure she wanted to risk destroying her dreams. She was, she acknowledged silently, suffering from an advanced case of creative cold feet.

"The sketches aren't finished," she said quickly. "They need hours more work before they'll be ready to submit for commercial appraisal."

"I realize that some of the drawings are still in preliminary stages. Don't worry, Linda, I'm not expecting perfection."

She should have known Matt wasn't the sort to be put off by a polite excuse. Adhering to social conventions had never been high on his list of priorities, particularly where art was concerned. Even as a teenager, he had been single-minded about his painting, which was one of the reasons Coach Mackenzie disliked him so much. The coach had offered Matt a position as starting quarterback on the high school football team Matt's senior year, and Matt had turned the offer down, explaining casually that football practice interfered with his art classes in Grand Junction.

Linda ventured the question she had been wanting to ask all night. "How about you, Matt? Have you managed to keep up with your painting?"

"Sort of." His tone of voice forbade further questions. He slanted a look toward her. "And don't change the subject, Lindy Beth. We're talking about you, not me. I asked if I could see your Rumbles drawings."

"How will you know if the patterns are workable? You don't have any experience in judging toy designs, do you?"

He hesitated for a moment. "No direct experience," he said finally. "I won't be a hundred percent sure if your work has real commercial potential, but I've hung around my friend when he's making this sort of decision, and I've got a fair idea of what he looks for. If I think your drawings look good, I'd mail them to my friend for his expert appraisal."

Linda concentrated on fastening the top button on Kate's sweater. "Maybe you'll think my whole concept for the Rumbles is lousy."

"It's possible," he agreed. "But wouldn't you like to have some idea whether you're working on next season's blockbuster toy, or indulging yourself in an interesting hobby?"

"I'm not sure," she admitted, surprising herself by her honesty. "Sometimes it's better to live in hope than to realize conclusively that you've failed."

"I know the feeling," he murmured.

He spoke with deep conviction, and she found herself remembering that by most people's standards, Matt himself was pretty much of a failure. At twenty-eight, he had no college degree, no job, no wife, no children, and presumably not much money. And yet, standing face to face with him, Linda felt that he radiated the sort of inner self-confidence that usually only accompanies major success. Whatever he'd made of his life so far, he seemed reasonably content with it.

His eyes were unexpectedly sympathetic as he looked down at her. He reached out and touched her very lightly on the cheek. "Why don't you think about it for a couple of days and call me if you decide you'd like me to take a look at your work? I'm going to be in town for a couple of weeks yet."

Before Linda could reply, the door was jerked open with an urgency that almost toppled her from her feet. Ron and Nora Owen stood framed in the doorway, Nora breathing deeply, as if she'd been hurrying.

Linda recovered her balance by grasping the doorjamb. "Mom! Dad! I didn't expect you home this early."

"No, I can see you didn't." Nora sounded more than usually repressive.

Ron cleared his throat. "Evenin', Matt," he said. "I guess I'll take care of Drew now." He reached out and transferred the sleeping child into his arms. "It's past time for the babies to be in bed," he explained, patting Drew with clumsy affection when he started to wriggle. Meanwhile, Nora Owen had requisitioned Kate, and was looking reproachfully at her daughter.

"It's nearly nine o'clock, Linda, two hours past their bedtime. Children of their age need a routine. You were always in bed by seven right through grade school, and never a murmur or a word of complaint out of you."

"It's summer," Linda said apologetically. "And they were having such a good time at the Deightons'. They can sleep late tomorrow."

"Are you coming in?" Nora asked, pointedly excluding Matt from her suggestion.

Matt straightened up from the porch post he'd been lolling against and draped his arm casually around Linda's shoulders. "No, thanks," he said with a genial smile. "It isn't our bedtime yet."

Nora Owen stared at his fingers, which were curled possessively around her daughter's arm, and gave every indication of imminent apoplexy. "Good heavens, Matt, the porch light's on!" she gasped. "Anybody could see you!"

"Could they?" Matt appeared supremely unconcerned by Nora's revelation. He glanced over his shoulder as if checking for spectators, then drew Linda even closer to his side. He looked down at her, creating a totally false impression of intimacy, and she saw the laughter dancing in his eyes—along with just a trace of anger. "We really appreciate you folks taking care of the twins and seeing them settled for the night, don't we, honey?"

"Yes, we do." As soon as she'd spoken the words, she wondered if Matt had hypnotized her. Why else had she agreed with this man who was deliberately poking fun at her parents' rigid standards?

He turned back to the Owens and gave them another laconic smile. "I guess Linda and I will take a stroll into town. If we happen to be late back, don't you folks bother to wait up. You can be sure I'll see she gets safely to bed."

Linda and her parents were all struck equally speechless by this seemingly ingenuous remark. Matt turned to walk away, but he didn't loosen his grip on Linda's shoulders; so she either had to demand her release or go meekly with him. She chose to accompany him down the steps, ignoring the strangled gasps of dismay that followed their progress along the path.

Her parents were acting as though she'd painted herself scarlet and declared her intention of walking naked through town, Linda thought ruefully. Just recently, she'd begun to realize that the people of Carson were determined to turn her into a living monument to Jim's heroic memory. The townsfolk in general, and her parents in particular, enjoyed having her slotted neatly into a permanent role as the town's "tragic young widow." If she allowed Carson to have its way, she'd soon feel guilty every time she spoke to an unmarried man. It was past time to strike this tiny blow for independence.

Matt strolled along, humming beneath his breath, seemingly without a care in the world. Linda breathed in the cool, dry air of the Colorado night and realized that, far from feeling annoyed at his outrageous behavior, she was fighting an almost irresistible urge to giggle. He'd always had this perverse capacity for making her see the ridiculous side of things. Maybe that's why her little act of defiance felt so good.

He dropped his arm from her shoulder as soon as they reached the street, and she told herself she was grateful for his consideration. She adjusted the cuffs on her blouse and tucked her hair back into its barrette. Heaven forbid that Mrs. Wittmeyer or any of her gossiping cronies should observe the widowed Mrs. James Petrie walking with her head nestled against Matt Deighton's shoulder. Carson would feast on a tidbit like that for weeks.

They continued in a surprisingly companionable silence until they reached the intersection with Main Street; then Matt asked her softly, "Want an ice cream?"

In the darkness, Linda felt her cheeks grow hot, which she knew was an absurd reaction to such a simple question. Matt probably didn't even remember that the first time he'd asked her out for ice cream had also been the first time they'd ever kissed. Why would he remember something so trivial? Their summer romance, etched with such dazzling luminescence into her memory, probably carried no more weight for Matt than a blurred, half-forgotten snapshot. Carson gossips never reported anything about Matt's life in New York, except that his tracks were littered by the broken hearts of the women he'd discarded.

She smiled up at him, forcing the bittersweet images

from her mind. "Are you good for a chocolate fudge ripple sundae?"

"Sure am. It sounds irresistible."

"But only a single. I already ate a slice of your mom's apple cake for dessert."

"You don't have to worry. You're thinner than you were at eighteen."

"I lost a lot of weight when . . . when Jim died. So far, I haven't gained all of it back."

Matt didn't look at her when he spoke. "Does it still hurt a lot?"

"Not as much as it used to."

He took her hand. "I'm sorry, Linda," he said softly.

She forced a bright smile. "Here's Scoop-a-Doop. What do you think of the snazzy new awning?"

"I think it's snazzy."

The ice-cream parlor was empty of customers, and Michelle Jones, one of this year's high school seniors, jumped up to serve them as soon as they walked in. She smiled at Linda and gave Matt a swift, interested appraisal. Her eyes lingered approvingly on his highly visible chest muscles, even when she spoke to Linda. "Hi, Mrs. Petrie, we haven't seen you in a while. Where are the twins?"

"They're at home with my parents."

Michelle reached for her scoop, her eyes roaming from Matt's chest muscles up to his rugged, cleft chin. "You've never been here without the twins before, Mrs. Petrie. Is it a special occasion?"

"They let her stay out late tonight as a reward for good behavior," Matt interjected smoothly. "Could you make us two chocolate fudge ripple sundaes, please? Singles."

The high school student piled ice cream into cardboard dishes, adding hot fudge sauce with a practiced flourish. "You visiting Carson?" she asked Matt politely when he handed over the money. "Not much to see around here. Most people head on south or into Utah."

"I'm visiting my family," Matt said, pocketing his change. "They live here in town. I'm Matthew Deighton."

"Matthew Deighton!" Michelle's eyes became round with awe. The scandal surrounding Matt's departure from Carson had by now mellowed sufficiently to take on all the overtones of a legend. In a town where buying a new brand of lawn fertilizer was hot news, the Mackenzie/Deighton saga was the closest Carson had come to producing its very own soap opera.

"I heard tell you were back in town," Michelle said, handing over the sundaes. "But I didn't realize Mrs. Petrie was a friend of yours." The girl didn't even try to hide her astonishment that the virtuous widow of the town hero would be keeping company with Carson's most infamous villain.

Matt gave the girl a smile that by some mysterious alchemy combined paternal amusement and blatant sexuality in almost equal proportions. "Even the Vestal Virgins were allowed to converse with male interlopers a couple of times a year."

Michelle, who had no idea who or what the Vestal Virgins might have been, smiled uncertainly. Matt handed Linda her sundae. "Ready?" he asked softly, his gaze locking with hers.

At some point, the paternal amusement had disappeared from his expression, leaving only the blatant sexuality. Linda stared up at him, hot fudge sauce dripping unheeded onto her fingers. She reached hastily for a napkin, transfixed by a welter of emotions, most of which were too complex to identify.

"Er . . . yes. Ready." Strange that she had never before noticed how difficult it was to breathe and eat ice cream at the same time.

"Let's go to the park, shall we?" he asked when they came out of the shop.

"The park would be fine."

There weren't too many places to go in Carson, but Linda began to wonder if it was entirely coincidence that Matt was choosing to retrace the identical route they'd taken on their very first date. "Why did you come home?" she asked as they crossed the railroad tracks. "I mean, why right at this moment?"

He took a lick of ice cream before replying. "Several reasons, but chiefly because I caught pneumonia earlier this year, and I couldn't seem to shake the after-effects. Anyway, my doctor kept threatening to hospitalize me if I didn't take a break. Coming home seemed like the best way to rest up."

"I'm sorry, you must have had a rough time. It can't be easy to look for work in construction when you're not feeling up to par."

He glanced at her rather oddly. "Who carried the news that I was unemployed back to town?"

"Mrs. Wittmeyer, of course, who else?"

"And, of course, her information's never wrong."

Linda laughed ruefully. "Mrs. Wittmeyer *wrong?* You've got to be kidding, Matt."

He licked his spoon. "I'd forgotten her reputation. Anyway, I'm glad to be home for a while, and the pneumonia is really no more than an excuse. I haven't seen enough of my parents these past few years."

They entered the small park and, without thinking, Linda sat down on the bench opposite a reservoir of water that the townsfolk proudly termed "the lake." Out-of-town visitors who were crass enough to refer to it as a pond soon had their mistake corrected.

"What happened to the ducks?" Matt asked, sitting beside her and stretching his long legs out in front of him.

"They're still here. Don't you remember? We never could see them at night."

"I'd forgotten that, too. Ducks weren't high on my list of interests when we used to come here. Deciding how many times I could kiss you before I exploded from frustration occupied most of my available brainpower."

Linda wasn't prepared for the angry question that burst out of her. "Is that why you went straight to Suzanne Mackenzie's apartment every time you left me?"

There was a slight pause. "Not every time," he replied eventually. "Very rarely, in fact. She was in need of a friend at the time."

Linda swallowed her final bite of ice cream. "Well, all those things happened a long time ago," she said, embarrassed by her unusual display of emotion. She normally prided herself on her calm, easy manner no matter what the provocation. It was ridiculous to let the events of a distant summer provoke her into being rude. She deliberately took refuge in one of the clichés she found so helpful in covering her true feelings. "Anyway, a lot of water's flowed under the bridge since then."

"I guess it has. In those days, there still seemed a pretty good chance you'd find the courage to set yourself free."

The anger flowed back in full force. "Free from what?" she demanded tightly.

"Carson."

"This may be a small town, but it isn't a prison, you know."

"For you it is. You're living the life your parents and

the local busybodies mapped out for you, not the life you'd have picked yourself if you'd really been free to choose."

"That's ridiculous. Just because I didn't go away to art school when you thought I should—"

"How is it ridiculous? From what I've seen, I'd say you couldn't even change your hairstyle without first asking permission from all seven hundred and fifty citizens of Carson."

"Seven hundred and fifty four," she corrected with a tiny smile. "We're having a baby boom."

"Doesn't it bother you to have your life controlled by public opinion?"

"I don't agree that it is."

"Even the high school kid in the ice-cream parlor was shocked that you came out without the twins as chaperons."

"That's because I was with you. Your family's provided Carson with some of our most exciting melodramas."

"No," he replied. "She was shocked even before she knew who I was. She was shocked because the beautiful widow of the Reverend Petrie was out with a man. Think about it, Linda. You probably have another sixty years of active life ahead of you. How many of those years are you willing to spend enshrined as a walking memorial to Jim Petrie?"

His question came uncomfortably close to some of the questions she'd recently been asking herself. "There are always trade-offs," she said finally. "People take a genuine interest in their neighbors in this part of the world. In Manhattan, you could be murdered in your bed and nobody would notice for a week. Here, a would-be murderer couldn't pass the town limits before somebody asked him what he was doing and how long he planned to stay. When people care about you, of course they're curious to know what you're doing."

"And when curiosity turns into interference, or into a witch-hunt, what then?"

Linda stared down at her tightly clasped hands. "If we're talking about what happened to you that summer, Matt, I know you were treated badly. Especially by me. I've often wanted to apologize to you for not speaking up. My only excuse is that I was very young. And scared."

He ran his hands through his hair, his voice sounding suddenly weary. "I knew what sort of pressure you were under, and I realized your parents wanted you to keep silent. You don't have to apologize."

"If the police had ever laid formal charges, I would have spoken up, I swear it, Matt. I hope you believe that."

He crooked his finger under her chin and turned her head slowly toward him. He gazed in silence into her eyes for a long time. "I think I believe you," he said at last.

"You're more generous than I deserve. Thank you." Her words hung in the air between them, expanding until they seemed to fill the narrow space separating their bodies. His eyes darkened and he leaned toward her, cupping her face with his hands.

"You still have the most kissable lips I've ever seen," he murmured, and his mouth touched hers in a light, fleeting kiss.

She felt the involuntary response that trembled through her body and knew that he felt it, too. His arms tightened around her waist, and he gathered her against his chest, kissing her with a passion that denied the long years of their separation. She kept her lips tightly closed, but he teased her with his tongue, brushing her mouth enticingly until she was tormented by the longing to surrender. Desire, more quickly aroused now than it had been when she had been a mere eighteen, coiled tight and demanding in the pit of her stomach. His hand slid over her thin blouse, and she fought to resist the shiver of pleasure his touch aroused. She would be crazy to give in to the demands of her body. Matt Deighton had caused her enough heartache. If she had a grain of sense, she wouldn't allow him to breeze into her well-ordered life and create another few weeks of havoc before he galloped off into the Manhattan sunset.

Resistance, however, was much easier to decide upon than to put into practice, and it was some considerable time later that she finally pulled herself out of Matt's arms.

"Mmm..." he said softly, smiling with infuriating complacence. "You taste even better than I remembered. I've been waiting seven years for that kiss."

"Poor you," she replied tartly. "I certainly hope it was worth the wait."

He grinned. "Nope. I'm afraid your technique's gotten a bit rusty. But don't worry, sweetheart, we'll work on it till you get it right."

She actually returned his smile until she realized that if she had a brain cell still functioning, she'd be hopping mad at his arrogance. "Don't hold your breath," she snapped.

He pretended to look shocked. "Of course not, honey. I learned how to breathe and kiss at the same time when *I* was a teenager."

She choked off a laugh and got up from the bench, abandoning the attempt to remain cross. Good grief, surely she hadn't turned into such a wizened old prune that she needed to make a big deal out of a kiss for old time's sake? "It's ten o'clock," she said. "I guess we ought to make tracks for home. Unfortunately, the twins think two minutes after sunrise is the perfect moment to start their day, and sunrise comes horribly early at this time of year."

He grinned. "I knew there was a good reason why I never had any children."

"Are you sure that you didn't?" She could have bitten off her tongue the moment she spoke.

The laughter faded from his expression. "Yes, I'm quite sure."

She clasped her hands so tightly together that the knuckles gleamed white. "I'm sorry. I had no right to ask you that question."

"Why not?" he said coolly. "Everyone else in Carson did, including the police."

"You never told them where you'd been that night, Matt. You never told them you'd been with me. Why not?"

He shrugged. "You were barely eighteen, and I'd just taken your virginity. Call it a residual sense of honor, if you like."

She avoided his gaze. "Were you having an affair with her, Matt?"

"You're not eighteen anymore, Linda—haven't you learned anything about men these past few years? How can you think I was capable of making love to you the way I did—of sharing what we shared—when I was having an affair with Suzanne Mackenzie?"

She stared unseeingly into the darkness. "I thought I was pregnant, you know. For two whole weeks while everybody was accusing you of being the father of Suzanne's baby, I thought I was pregnant, too."

He was silent for so long, she thought he might not respond at all. "Why the hell didn't you tell me?" he said at last.

Her smile was bitter. "What would you have done? Offered to marry me? I knew you better than that, Matt."

"Did you? I've often wondered if we knew each other at all. Dammit, Linda, if you were pregnant, the responsibility was mine. You were so naive, I don't think you knew what birth control was. And yet you let me leave Carson without saying a word!"

"By the time you left, I knew it had been a false alarm."

He shoved his hands into the pockets of his jeans. "For what it's worth, I swear I wasn't the father of Suzanne Mackenzie's baby, Linda. Our affair finished three months before I started dating you."

She had a sudden insight. "But you know who the father of her baby was, don't you, Matt?"

He shrugged. "Yeah, I know."

"Will you tell me?"

"Why not? I guess it doesn't matter anymore. It was the high school principal."

"Aaron Beckworth? Goodness gracious, Matt, why ever didn't you speak up?"

"That was in my noble days," he said, his voice mocking. "Besides, he had a wife and three kids. At the time, it seemed like a good idea to protect his family."

"He resigned and left town just after you did."

Matt skimmed a stone across the flat surface of the pond. "I suggested to him that would be a smart move on his part if he wanted me to keep quiet."

Linda watched the stone skip into the distance, then sink into the darkness of the water. "Carson locked you up in your role just as tight as I was locked up in mine," she said. "You were the official bad boy, and when you protected me and Suzanne and the Beckworths, nobody said thank you. You just got drummed out of town for your pains."

"And you lied about what we'd been doing that night, and the town rewarded you by adding another layer of gold to your halo. I wonder which of us got the better deal?"

Linda was afraid to answer that question. She was almost sure she didn't want to hear her own answer.

Chapter Three

FOR THIRTY-EIGHT years, Nora Owen had served coffee, cinnamon rolls, and gossip in her parlor on the first Monday morning of each month. This Monday in June was no exception. Indeed, the return of Matthew Deighton promised to enliven the gathering with the heady spice of fresh scandal. Linda knew that despite all her worries about Lindy Beth and That Man, Nora was actually looking forward to her party.

Carrying a tray of cake, she hurried out of the kitchen to join the dozen women assembled in her living room with her daughter. She put down the heavy tray on a lace-covered table, smothering a smile. This party was going to put Greta Wittmeyer's nose sorely out of joint. There was a certain reflected glory in being the hostess of a coffee party when a juicy item of gossip broke.

Nora, unfortunately, underestimated the opposition. Mrs. Wittmeyer possessed intelligence-gathering skills that left the average FBI operative looking like a rank amateur, and she had no intention of allowing her life-long rival to achieve a social coup. She accepted a cup of coffee from Linda and smiled, displaying the full glory of her false teeth. Linda recognized the sharklike qualities of the smile and mentally stiffened.

Mrs. Wittmeyer attacked while still stirring cream

41

into her coffee. "I hear you and Matthew Deighton were out together last night, Lindy Beth. I expect he's learned all sorts of fancy tricks since he went to New York. And such a *handsome* man! He's enough to turn any woman's head."

Linda was surprised to discover she felt amused rather than flustered by this blatant assault. She produced her sunniest smile. "Yes, he is handsome, isn't he? I think he's even better-looking now than when he left Carson."

A shocked and interested silence greeted her reply. Linda deftly removed Drew's fingers from the sugar bowl and spoke into the silence. "If you sit down, Drew honey, I'll get you a cookie and a cup of milk."

Nora Owen wasn't wise enough to let well enough alone. "Lindy Beth wasn't *out* with Matthew," she said, her voice betraying her agitation. "She would never *go out* with a man like that. They were just...just... together."

"Is that so?" Eyes gleaming, Mrs. Wittmeyer delicately returned her cup to her saucer. "Is that what the two of you were doing in the park, Lindy Beth? Just being—together?"

Linda's earlier amusement vanished. "Yes," she replied curtly. "We bought ice-cream sundaes and spent a few minutes catching up on old times while we ate."

Once again, Nora rushed foolishly to her daughter's rescue. "There was never anything at all between that dreadful man and Lindy Beth," she asserted fiercely. "Nothing at all."

Mrs. Wittmeyer's eyebrows raised. "My dear, I never suspected for one minute that there was. We all know what a model teenager Lindy Beth was. Why in the world are you looking so hot and bothered, Nora, dear?"

"Do you remember when Matt made the winning touchdown in the final game of the season?" Becky Weaver interjected hastily, addressing the room at large. "He was only a junior, and how far did he run? Forty yards, wasn't it?"

"Forty-seven," Linda replied absently, her attention fixed on Kate, who was trying to drink the jug of coffee creamer. "It was a state record."

Mrs. Wittmeyer fanned herself with a paper napkin. "My goodness, Nora, how amazingly *well* Lindy Beth remembers all these little details about Matthew Deighton!"

Becky sprang to her feet. "More coffee anyone? You just make the best coffee of anybody in town, Nora."

"Thanks, I'd love some more." Barb Jamison held out her cup. "Matt never played football during his senior year, did he? I often wondered why Coach Mackenzie wouldn't have him back on the team."

"Matt was taking art classes after school," Linda said shortly. "It wasn't that the coach didn't want him on the team."

"That's one version of the story," Mrs. Wittmeyer remarked smugly. "But I've heard another, more interesting, one."

Linda felt her cheeks flame. She stood up, grasping Kate in one hand and Drew in the other. "You always have heard something more interesting, haven't you, Mrs. Wittmeyer? But do you ever care if your version happens to be true?"

When Linda realized what she'd said, she couldn't believe it. From the stunned looks coming from her mother's guests, she deduced that they couldn't believe it either. She retreated to the door, appalled at having created a scene in her mother's living room.

"I'm sorry, Mrs. Wittmeyer. Excuse me, please,

ladies. I have to take Kate and Drew outside to help my father in the yard."

It was a relief to walk out into the dry, Colorado sunshine. Her father had taken the day off from work and was digging in his vegetable patch. "Horrible the way these weeds grow," he remarked cheerfully, making no reference to the *kaffeklatsch* going on inside the house. "You two planning to help?" he asked the twins.

"Yes," they said simultaneously.

Ron eased himself down to the twins' height, then pointed to a tray of seedlings. "One day, those will grow up to be carrots. You have to dig a hole like this with your trowel, then you plant a baby carrot inside each hole and fill the hole up again with soil. The soil is food for the seedling, to make it grow."

"Like cookies for us," Kate said, pleased with the thought.

"Sort of," Linda agreed. "More like milk or juice."

Drew and Kate ignored their mother's lesson in nutrition. They dug eagerly and with no skill at all until they had produced several shallow troughs in the earth. "Very good," Ron said, handing them each a seedling. "Now plant these just like I showed you."

Drew frowned in concentration, his tongue sticking out of the corner of his mouth as he struggled to get the fragile plant positioned correctly. Kate tossed her plant into the nearest hole and scattered earth over it, indifferent to its drunken tilt.

"Done," she said. "More carrots, Grandpa."

"You haven't got it quite right," Ron explained patiently. "Look, Katie, you have to support the plant with the earth, or it'll die before the roots get strong enough to hold it. Like this, Katie."

"You never used to let me help you in the garden." Linda flushed as soon as the accusatory words left her mouth. It was the second time in fifteen minutes that she had spoken first and thought second. Usually, she went for weeks at a stretch without making a single unconsidered remark. She couldn't imagine what had come over her in the past twenty-four hours.

Her father stood up, dusting his hands on the seat of his gardening pants. "Your mother didn't like you to get dirty," he said after a pause. "And I went along with her. You were so pretty, you know, Lindy Beth. Just like a picture on a calendar." He cleared his throat. "You still are. Pretty, I mean."

"She sure is," said a voice from the fence. "I can never work out why I don't hate her. Must be my supernice nature, I guess. Any intelligent woman would have more sense than to stay friends with somebody who looks like Miss America."

"Jennifer!" Linda swung around, her mouth breaking into a smile. She put her hands on her hips and laughed. "Any special reason why you're squirming in the bushes?"

"A damn good reason. I'm stuck. Whatever happened to the gap we always used?"

"Either it shrank or you expanded."

"Bite your tongue. A TV anchorwoman *never* expands."

Linda laughed again. "Then, obviously, the gap must have shrunk. Are you planning to spend the morning hanging halfway into our yard, or would you like some help?"

"You could hold on to these darn branches, so I don't totally destroy my new pants when I wriggle through."

Linda obligingly held the branches, and her friend emerged panting onto the Owens' side of the fence.

"Hi Ron. Hi kids." Jennifer carelessly plucked twigs from her muslin blouse. The thin fabric revealed the fact that she wore no bra, and no camisole either. Linda couldn't tell whether or not her friend's pants had survived the journey through the bushes unscathed. They looked tattered enough to have been rescued from a Salvation Army clothing dump, but she suspected their mangy appearance merely proved how expensive they were.

"Pants okay?" she asked, not hiding her amusement.

Jennifer glanced down. "More or less."

"I'm glad. They're very New York. A shade of khaki that revolting must have cost a fortune."

Jennifer grinned. "It did." She wiped her hands over the front of her blouse, giving up on the twig removal. "I loathe this outfit anyway. I can't imagine why I bought it." She ran scarlet-painted nails through her hair, which had once been mousey brown and was now gleaming auburn. "The yard's beautiful, Ron, and you're looking in terrific shape yourself."

"Thanks, I can't complain."

Jennifer knelt between the twins. "What are you planting?"

"Vegabuls," Drew replied. "Big vegabuls."

"Carrots," Kate elucidated.

"Mmm . . . my favorites. When they're grown, will you save some for me?"

"All of them," said Drew with one of his rare and charming smiles. "I hate vegabuls," he added.

"But these vegetables will taste special, because you grew them yourselves. You'll see. You'll love these carrots."

"If they ever get planted," Ron said. "We'd better get busy." Eyes twinkling, he looked at Jennifer. "Did you come over to help?"

"I came over to beg a cup of Nora's coffee. I'd forgotten how awful my mother's brew tastes, and I can only make the instant stuff."

"Mom's having one of her parties," Linda interjected hastily. "Mrs. Wittmeyer and her cronies are out in full force. If you venture into the living room, they'll all be waiting to pounce."

"Right now, I'd brave a dozen Mrs. Wittmeyers for a cup of decent coffee." Jennifer linked her arm through Linda's and marched determinedly toward the house. "Bye kids. Bye Ron. Nice to see you again."

"I'll make you coffee in the kitchen," Linda volunteered once they were out of her father's earshot.

"Are you chicken, Lindy Beth? Scared to go into the parlor with the grown-ups?"

"You betcha. Mrs. Wittmeyer's eagle eye is enough to turn any smart person chicken."

Jennifer grinned. "Heck, with me in the room, they won't give you a second glance. Mrs. Wittmeyer will be so busy trying to decide if she can really see my nipples, she won't even notice you're there."

Linda's laughter sounded wistful. "I don't think I could even say the word *nipple* to anybody except you, and maybe my doctor. Why don't people intimidate you, Jennifer?"

"They do, sometimes, if I respect them. But not the Mrs. Wittmeyers of the world. She's too petty."

"She's not petty. She's *avid*. She spends her time sucking all the tiny, secret details of your life out of you. Then she churns them around inside her head and makes them into something nasty. How can you ignore her?"

"Part of the reason I went to New York was to get away from Mrs. Wittmeyer and her cronies."

"But you're here today, and so is she. Why doesn't she bother you?"

"Because I let her find out all the things that don't matter. While she's worrying about my nipples and my dyed hair, she forgets to poke about inside me. She can complain all she wants about my body, so long as she leaves my soul alone."

"It's an intriguing thought," Linda muttered, pausing at the kitchen sink to rinse her hands. "Somehow, though, I can't imagine myself buying a see-through blouse, much less wearing it to one of Carson's coffee parties. The widowed Mrs. James Petrie in transparent muslin. Can you visualize the Reverend Dunning's face when he heard about it? Not to mention my mother's."

Jennifer's voice was quiet. "Linda, when are you going to stop living to please other people? It doesn't work in the end, you know. You end up annoying everybody, especially yourself."

"You and your brother seem to be reading from the same script," Linda muttered.

"I didn't realize Matt had so much good sense. I hope he told you that you can't make yourself over into somebody you're not, however hard you try. You aren't quite the meek-and-mild semivirgin Carson would like you to be."

"I'm not trying to make myself over," Linda protested, ignoring the remark about semivirgins. "I know who I am."

"Who?"

"Well, I'm the twins' mother. And Jim's widow, of course."

"You're also a young and beautiful woman."

Linda's hands clenched on the kitchen towel. "By the calendar, I may be young. Sometimes I feel a hundred years old."

Jennifer smiled wryly. "That, my dear, sweet Lindy Beth, is precisely the problem. You act as if you're a hundred, and your parents treat you as if you were ten. It's about time somebody in this town remembered that you're a functioning female of twenty-five."

Linda forced a laugh. "I can hear it coming, Jen. You're about to launch into one of your sex-is-the-answer-to-everything lectures."

"You never could get it right, Lindy Beth. *Sex* isn't the answer to anything. *Good sex* is what you need."

Linda's cheeks grew pink. "You know what? Mrs. Wittmeyer and my mother's parlor are beginning to look better and better. Want to come and get that cup of coffee?"

Ten of the original twelve guests were still chatting in the living room when Linda escorted her friend into the room. All ten sparked up immediately when they recognized Jennifer. A chorus of greetings rang out.

"Hi, folks, nice to see you all." Jennifer smiled at the hostess. "I've come to beg a cup of your special coffee, Nora. Mom brewed her usual offering of coal-tar and then took off for her studio."

"You mean she's out in the garage again?" Mrs. Wittmeyer asked. "Lord bless me, I've never known a woman to spend so much time in a garage."

"We don't have a garage," Jennifer replied softly. "My mother's in her *studio*, working on a new design for a coffeepot. It was commissioned by a major manufacturing firm in Boston."

"That's wonderful," Mrs. Wittmeyer said. "Everybody knows how hard Sally worked to build up her little hobby. We can all understand that she didn't have as much time to spend with her children as the rest of us. We can't expect every mother to put her children's well-being ahead of her own interests."

"No, we can't," Jennifer replied with her sweetest

smile. "But don't worry, Mrs. Wittmeyer. I'm sure your children don't hold your behavior against you."

"Here, my dear, have some coffee," Nora interjected quickly, drowning out a gurgle of laughter from Becky Weaver. She clearly wasn't quite sure whether to feel delighted or worried at having Jennifer in her living room. On the one hand, Jennifer's presence crowned her party with unexpected glory. On the other hand, her presence might tempt people to return to unwelcome subjects— subjects like Matthew Deighton, for example.

"When are you starting work?" Nora asked, attempting to head off danger. "We were thrilled to hear you'd been recruited by Channel Ten in Denver. The TV critics all say they have the best local news shows."

"I think so, too," Jennifer agreed, sipping her coffee. "I'm starting next week, and I'm excited about getting this chance to anchor one of their broadcasts, even though I'll have to be up at four in the morning. Unfortunately, they start the rookies on the six A.M. breakfast program."

Talk centered for several minutes on Jennifer's career in TV journalism, and Linda curled up in a corner, listening intently. Her friend's ambition and hard work never failed to impress her, and she wasn't surprised that Jennifer had succeeded in such a tough, competitive field.

A momentary lull in the conversation gave Mrs. Wittmeyer the chance she must have been waiting for. She aimed her deadliest smile in Jennifer's direction. "I hear you and Doug Hotchkiss were sharing a candlelight dinner in Grand Junction the other night. We never knew he was a special friend of yours."

Linda glanced quickly across the room, torn between surprise and amusement. Doug Hotchkiss? Jennifer had been dining with Doug, of all people?

Jennifer returned her cup to its saucer with a tiny clatter. "Doug?" she said, a little too carelessly. Linda wondered if she was the only person to notice the telltale tensing of her friend's body. "Oh, you're talking about our business meeting on Thursday evening. Doug's the senior computer consultant at Channel Ten, you know, and he works on all the graphics for the news programs. If you're fascinated by bytes, rams, and megachips he makes the perfect dinner companion. Otherwise..." Her voice trailed off and she rolled her eyes heavenward.

Most of the women laughed, as Jennifer had clearly intended, and talk turned to the amazing success Doug Hotchkiss had made of his company, now one of the largest employers in Grand Junction.

Linda watched as her friend strolled over to the coffeepot and poured herself another cup. Jennifer seemed totally unconcerned, but Linda thought she could detect just a trace of red creeping into her friend's cheeks. Linda could scarcely believe that a woman as sophisticated as Jennifer Deighton was blushing over Doug Hotchkiss. Doug had been honored in his high school yearbook with the well-deserved title *Nerd of the Year*. The last time Linda had seen him, admittedly several years ago, he still hadn't grown into his horn-rimmed glasses, and his manner had varied between shy and totally tongue-tied.

An excited muttering snapped Linda's attention back into focus. Like every other woman in the room, she found herself staring toward the door, where Matthew Deighton, all six feet two inches of him, leaned comfortably. He wore the inevitable pair of faded jeans, and a cotton shirt flapping at his waist. Whenever he moved, the shirt flopped open to reveal a swathe of muscular chest. Linda suddenly found herself wondering what good sex felt like.

"Hello, ladies, how are you doing?" Matt's husky voice seemed to dissolve the common sense of most of the women in the room. Even Mrs. Wittmeyer looked dreamy-eyed for a second or two. Only Nora Owen, ever vigilant in protection of her daughter, displayed her usual frown.

"I didn't hear you knock," she said dourly.

Matt smiled with breathtaking charm. "I didn't knock, Nora. Ron let me in. He's taken the twins upstairs for a quick shower."

"Did you want to speak to Jennifer?"

Matt's amused gaze traveled toward his sister. "Not particularly. We ate breakfast together without exchanging a single cross word, and I'd hate to ruin such a spectacular achievement."

Jennifer laughed. "Let me guess. Did you come in search of decent coffee, big brother?"

"No," he said calmly. "I came in search of Linda. I'd like to spend the afternoon with her, and I thought we could take the kids on a picnic to Benton Reservoir."

One dozen pairs of fascinated eyes turned toward Linda. "She can't go!" Nora's voice wobbled alarmingly. "She has to clean her room, and the twins need a nap."

"They can sleep in the truck," Matt suggested. "I planned on taking my dad's Wagoneer." His blue eyes met Linda's with an intensity that belied his easy smile. "Want to come?" he asked softly. "You could always clean your room when we get home."

For the third time in one morning, Linda spoke without calculating the consequences. She rose to her feet and walked over to the door, her gaze locked with Matt's. "Thank you," she said. "I'd love to come."

Mrs. Wittmeyer was the first person to recover her voice. "Well!" she said. "Well, well, well. Whoever would've thought it?"

Chapter Four

MATT WASN'T SURE whether he or the ladies of Carson were more astonished when Linda accepted his invitation. If he was honest, he'd have to admit he asked her out more to annoy Nora Owen than because he really wanted to spend time with Linda. The way their relationship had ended didn't exactly make for easy revivals of old friendship.

Nevertheless, he found himself oddly touched as Linda ran the gauntlet of a dozen interested stares to walk over and join him. She appeared coolly unaware of the disapproving murmurs that followed her progress, but Matt could see otherwise. The top button of her shirt was unfastened and the pulse throbbing in her throat betrayed just how difficult she found it to publicly accept an invitation from Carson's most infamous black sheep.

Smiling a mocking good-bye to the gawking ladies, Matt put his hand against the small of Linda's back and urged her toward the stairs. He was suddenly anxious to protect her from the probing glances of the gossip hounds, not to mention Nora Owen's biting tongue. For himself, he didn't care what they said. Having survived small-town gossip at its most vindictive, he no longer minded in the slightest what people like Mrs. Wittmeyer chose to report about him. In a few days, two weeks at most, he would be leaving Carson, and he would once again tuck everything about this place into some unimportant, faraway corner of his mind.

However, he'd grown up here, so he understood that Linda's situation differed quite a bit from his own. Her role as Jim Petrie's widow made her fair game for the most intense scrutiny. The smallest slip left her vulnerable to attack by every armchair moralist. The townsfolk of Carson had put her on a pedestal, and they couldn't make up their minds whether they wanted to keep her there or pull her down and gloat over the crash. To his surprise, no matter how badly she'd treated him in the past, Matt discovered that he didn't want to contribute to Linda's downfall.

"I thought we could buy some fried chicken on the way out of town," he said, pausing at the foot of the stairs. "Do you want to collect what you need for the twins, while I get my father's truck?"

"Sounds good," she said, not looking at him. She hadn't actually looked at him since she'd agreed to come on the picnic. "The twins and I have a weakness for the colonel's extra-crispy drumsticks."

"Extra crispy it will be. Don't forget to bring your swimsuits."

"Swimsuits? Matt, the water'll be freezing!"

"Freezing may be what we need before the day's over."

Her hand clenched on the banister. "I doubt it," she said quietly. "We're both a lot older now."

He hadn't intended his words to carry a double meaning. He'd meant only that the afternoon temperature was likely to soar into the nineties. But her reply reminded him that they'd visited the reservoir before, in that long-ago summer when he'd imagined himself to be permanently, hopelessly in love.

Erotic memories unrolled in his mind, startling in their clarity. He could almost feel the grass tickling beneath his back, and smell the sun-warmed heat of her skin. Her girlish body had been light and immature in his arms, but he had shuddered with frustrated desire when her small breasts thrust against his chest. They'd had the place to themselves, so inevitably their love-making reached its usual pitch of mind-shaking, gut-wrenching intensity. Only a plunge into the ice-cold waters of the reservoir had prevented him from leading them both into disaster.

She was right, Matt thought, looking at the upswept neatness of her blond hair, and the ladylike pearl studs in her delicate earlobes. They *were* a lot older now. Meeting Linda nowadays, most men would think she'd never known the meaning of the word *passion*. As for himself . . . he couldn't remember when he'd last experienced the sort of feverish, all-consuming desire that had tormented him day after day, night after night, for that entire endless summer.

He thrust the memories aside and spoke with deliberate lightness. "Hey, we're not that old, are we? My bones may creak, but I can still swim, even in cold water."

His casualness seemed to relieve her. She smoothed the crease in her immaculate navy linen pants and ventured a small smile. "All right, then. We'll bring swim-suits. Does ten minutes sound okay?"

"Ten minutes it is. I'll meet you at the front gate."

He had another glimpse of her fleeting smile before she ran up the stairs, two at a time, calling for the twins. Her smile tugged at his emotions, and he tried to work out why. His taste in women these days ran to the dark and lush rather than the pale and repressed. Jennifer caught up with him before he had reached any conclusions.

"You certainly set the cat among the pigeons," she said as they turned into their parents' yard. "For a while there, I thought Mrs. Owen was going to choke on her own cinnamon cake, and as for Mrs. Wittmeyer . . . she was so excited she was speechless for five whole minutes."

Matt grinned. "In New York, I could bed four different women at once and nobody would know or care. Here, I can't even invite an old friend out for a picnic —with her kids in tow!—without the entire town going into a tailspin."

Jennifer raised an inquiring eyebrow. "Four women at once? Matt, I'm impressed."

He ruffled her hair. "Don't be more aggravating than you have to be, sweet. You know I was talking hypothetically."

"I couldn't be certain. Speaking as a sister who got sadly left out in the looks department, I'd say you're too damn sexy for your own good."

Matt reached into his jeans pocket for the keys to his father's truck. "If you only knew what a sober life I lead in Manhattan."

"I can guess," Jennifer said dryly. "Remember, I've met some of your harem." Without giving her brother a chance to reply, she spoke again. "Linda is my best friend, Matt. She's had some hellish bad luck. Don't hurt her."

He frowned as he opened the truck door. "Jen, you know me better than that. I'm twenty-eight years old, for heaven's sake, and I compete in Manhattan's toughest industry. I don't need to seduce innocents like Linda to prove to myself that I'm a man."

"A man doesn't always have to take a woman to bed in order to hurt her."

"I'm flattered, Jen, but I'm sure you're vastly over-estimating my appeal to Linda."

Uncharacteristically, Jennifer stared at the ground. "That summer before you left home...before all the mess with Suzanne Mackenzie...anybody with half an eye could have seen Linda was head over heels in love with you. But I always thought you were in love with her, too. Nobody else seems to have noticed that."

Matt swung into the truck and slammed the door. "Jen, stop worrying. I'm not suffering from some post-adolescent hangup on your friend Linda. If I feel anything at all for her, it's pity. She's so hemmed in by all the old biddies in this town, it makes me claustrophobic just to watch."

"It's her mother who's the real problem," Jennifer said seriously. "Nora was childless for fourteen years, and then this perfectly beautiful baby arrived in the arms of the adoption caseworker. Nora's been terrified of losing her daughter ever since."

Matt turned on the ignition. "I agree, but I'm not sure what any of us can do about the situation. Only Linda can solve that problem, and she doesn't want to. I have to go, Jen, unless you want to come with me and act as chaperon?"

She stuck her hands into her pants pockets. "Er... no...thanks all the same. I have an...um...meeting this afternoon in Grand Junction."

He put the truck into reverse. "Have fun."

"Sure. And Matt—you take care you don't have too much."

Linda and the twins were walking down the path as he drew up outside the gate to her parents' house. The twins looked cool and comfortable in red shorts and sleeveless T-shirts. Linda had changed her navy linen pants for a pair of baggy cotton shorts and a beige cotton-knit top. Either item, Matt reflected, would have looked perfectly appropriate on a sixty-year-old grandmother. Didn't she ever wear any bright colors, or styles that flattered her long, slender body?

He put on the brake, feeling a spurt of anger. Who was she trying to impress by dressing herself up in such dowdy outfits? The townsfolk? Her parents? If she was trying to send him a hands-off message, she was wasting her time. He hadn't the faintest interest in going to bed with her, or even indulging in a few days' casual flirtation. Her face and figure might be spectacularly beautiful, but she exuded about as much sensuality as the average dressmaker's dummy. He wondered what had happened to all the fire and passion that had smoldered so close to the surface seven summers ago. No doubt it was buried with her hero husband in the town cemetery.

Matt got out of the truck, and Kate ran up to him, holding out a pint-sized straw bag for his inspection. Drew followed behind, lugging a plastic supermarket bag stuffed with a small pillow.

"Hi, Matt. Me and Drew is going swimming," Kate announced. She tossed a dismissive glance toward her brother. "Drew can't swim."

He scowled. "I *can* so swim. You can't."

Kate put her hands on her hips and glared at her brother. "I'm biggerer than you."

Matt laughed and scooped her up into his arms. He deposited her gently in the back of the Wagoneer. "What's your size got to do with anything, young lady?"

"I'm biggerer," Kate repeated stubbornly, nestling into her corner of the seat and arranging her bag on her lap.

Drew, still outside the Wagoneer, remained silent. Matt squatted down next to him. "Hey, old feller, you must stick up for your rights! You look just as big as Katie to me. In fact, you look taller than she is."

Drew stared gloomily at his sister. "She is biggerer," he said, and clambered into the truck, his pillow bouncing against his ankles.

Matt glanced at Linda in silent question as they adjusted the children's seat belts. "Kate was born fifteen minutes before Drew," she explained, swinging up into the front passenger seat. "They both seem to think that gives her a lifelong entitlement to superiority. I think Drew could be six inches taller and Katie would still claim she was bigger."

Matt set the Wagoneer in motion. "Hmm. The male chauvinist in me rebels at seeing Drew subjected to such an obvious power play. I'm going to have to work out some way to convince him that a fifteen-minute head-start on life isn't unconquerable."

Linda glanced back at the twins, who were taking off each other's shoes and paying no attention to the adult conversation. "It would be great if you could," she said. "I'm so used to seeing Kate in front and Drew following on behind that I don't make enough effort to break the pattern."

"I didn't intend to make a big deal out of nothing. For what my opinion's worth, they seem really well adjusted to me."

"I worry sometimes because they're twins. People always refer to them as if they were a single entity. *How are the twins today? Where are the twins? Do the twins want a cookie?* Nobody seems to realize that maybe Drew is fine, but Katie has a cold, or that one of them wants a cookie, but not the other."

"You're lucky they're not the same sex. Once they're

teenagers, I imagine they'll look quite different from each other. At the moment, they seem like male and female versions of the same person, which must affect how people behave toward them."

"They do look alike," Linda agreed. "They're the image of their father, both of them."

"Jim must have been very handsome if the twins take after him," Matt remarked.

"He was. Most people have some sort of a flaw—a crooked nose, or bushy eyebrows, or flapping ears. But Jim's features were all perfect."

Matt broke the momentary silence. "I didn't think you would want me at the funeral, Linda, or I'd have come home."

She stared out of the window, so that all he could see was her profile. "You wrote to me. I understood why you stayed away. Nobody could have made things any better at that point."

"Does it still hurt, Linda? Do you miss him a lot?" As soon as he'd spoken, Matt wished he could recall the question. He'd asked her this same question already, and she'd chosen not to answer. He had no justification for prying into the intimacy of Linda's feelings for her dead husband.

Her profile gave no clue at all as to what she was thinking, but when she spoke Matt could hear the throb of deep, painful emotion in her voice.

"Jim was the kindest, most generous man I've ever met," she said. "He worked sixty-hour weeks on behalf of the church, and still found time to help me with the twins. They were barely five pounds each when they were born, and they didn't sleep through the night for over four months. Jim knew the pregnancy had exhausted me, and he got up for the two A.M. feedings as often as I did. He would have been a terrific father. He made everybody around him feel . . . cherished."

"My parents told me how happy you were together, and what a great marriage you had. You lost a wonderful husband, Linda."

She closed her eyes, but not in time to catch the tears that trickled silently down her cheek.

Matt watched her distress, his throat aching. "I'm sorry," he murmured. "I'm really sorry, Linda."

She fished a handkerchief out of her pocket and pressed it to her eyes. Fortunately, Kate chose that precise moment to bop her brother over the head, and in the ensuing mayhem Linda's tears dried and she returned to her smiling self. By the time they stopped to pick up fried chicken for their picnic lunch, she was laughing as if their discussion of Jim Petrie had never happened.

Matt was parking the truck at the reservoir before he realized what had been nagging at him about their conversation. Although Linda had spoken willingly of Jim Petrie's many perfections, she had never actually answered Matt's original question. She had never actually said whether or not she missed her husband.

Jim Petrie sounded like such a paragon, Matt decided Linda's omission could only be accidental.

Linda pushed the last chicken bone into the cardboard carton, and wiped her fingers on one of the premoistened towelettes. She rolled over onto her stomach, and dropped her head onto her arms.

"Drew and Kate look like they're dissecting an anthill," Matt murmured. "Do you mind?"

"Yes, but I've eaten too much to move. Do you think they're the sort of ants that sting?"

"I have no idea, but I'll go check." He sighed with fake resignation, poking her gently in the ribs. "It's a good thing one of us knew when to stop eating. Are you going to be comatose for the rest of the afternoon?"

"Probably." She kept her head buried in her arms, pretending to be half-asleep. That way he couldn't see the wave of color that had swept into her cheeks when his thumb brushed against her breast. She felt his gaze rest on the nape of her neck for a few seconds before he pulled himself easily to his feet and strolled off toward the scrub oak.

When he was a safe distance away, she propped her chin on her hand, watching him as he bent down to examine the anthill with the twins. Linda wasn't surprised to see Kate welcome him with a beaming smile. Kate basically assumed everybody was her friend. Drew was another story altogether, and Linda felt a spurt of pleasure when she saw how relaxed her son looked as he tugged at Matt's arm to point out some special attraction of the ants' nest.

Her attention gradually wandered from the children and concentrated on Matt. His body showed the muscle-building effects of years working on construction jobs. His broad shoulders strained against the thin cotton of his shirt, and the corded muscles of his thighs made taut the faded denim of his jeans to produce an effect worthy of any TV commercial. Taken together with laughing blue eyes and a mouth that combined cynicism and tenderness in tantalizing proportions, Matthew Deighton's body packed an aggressive sexual punch. Even though he was temporarily unemployed, Linda had no doubt that he attracted all the women he wanted into his life and into his bed. In fact, he probably had volunteers for bedroom duty lined up along his apartment corridors.

Her stomach dipped in an odd, lurching sort of movement, and she sat up hurriedly, hugging her knees. Something strange was happening to her. She'd thought more about sex and men's bodies these past couple of days than she had in the whole of the last two years. This morning she'd even drawn a gingham-skirted female Rumble, with stubby paws clutched to its heart as it stared longingly at a top-hatted male Rumble striding off into the sunset. After nearly three years of celibacy, Linda wondered if her hormones had exploded into some bizarre form of overload.

Matt returned and dropped down onto the rug beside her. "It was a just regular old anthill," he said. "Not a warrior ant in sight. But I persuaded the twins they'd prefer to dig somewhere else until we can take them swimming."

She squinted into the sun, and saw the twins happily scooping sand into their beach pails. "They're usually more stubborn."

"I discovered they're as susceptible to bribes as the rest of us. I promised them giant ice-cream cones on the way home."

"Smart thinking," Linda said. She'd discovered that if she didn't look at him, she could keep her voice quite steady. Maybe she wasn't going into hormone overload after all. "You were right about the swimsuits, Matt. I'm glad we brought them. It's boiling hot out here, and I'm really looking forward to a dip later on."

"Why don't you take off your shorts and shirt if you're too hot?" Matt suggested.

"Er . . . what?"

"You'd be cooler in your swimsuit."

"I prefer to keep my clothes on, thanks." She swallowed hard. "I burn easily."

He didn't question the lie. "Poor you. I never have that problem, although my mother's always telling me horror stories about how I'll get skin cancer before I'm fifty."

"Mothers are obliged to tell horror stories, that's union rules. I always swore I wouldn't, but do you know, the other day I heard myself telling Kate that she'd never grow tall if she didn't eat her crusts. I almost bit off my tongue."

Matt chuckled. "Depressing how like our parents we turn out to be, isn't it?"

"Not all of us. You managed to break away."

"But my mother was always the town rebel. In a way, I'm following right in her footsteps."

Linda wasn't rude enough to point out that there were some big differences between Matt and his mother. Sally Deighton's rebellion was limited to designing teapots in a converted garage and refusing to provide cakes for the PTA bake sale. Matt had rebelled from the day he entered kindergarten, and had dropped out of school without graduating when a local sculptor offered him the chance to study art full time. In the end, after narrowly avoiding imprisonment on rape charges, he'd totally rejected the small-town lifestyle.

The sounds of Matt standing up penetrated Linda's reverie, and she forgot her determination not to look at him. She turned around just in time to see him toss his shirt onto the rug and start to unzip his jeans. Mesmerized, she watched as he stepped out of the jeans, revealing a dark blue nylon swimsuit that might as well have been painted onto his body for all the concealment it provided.

He sat down again on the rug. "I think another twenty minutes should do it, don't you?"

She reminded herself to breathe. "Tw-twenty minutes?"

"Before we can swim," he explained patiently.

She kept her gaze fixed rigidly forward. "Twenty minutes should be fine."

He stretched himself out on the rug, six feet two inches of perfect masculinity spread out for her inspection. Linda closed her eyes.

A shrill cry galvanized her into action. She sprang to her feet and tore across the grass to the sand where the twins were digging. "What is it, honey?" She pulled Kate into her arms. "What happened, sweetheart?"

Drew pointed to his sister's toe. "She's bloody."

Linda checked the broken nail on her daughter's big toe, and her heartbeat gradually returned to normal. Katie's cry had contained real pain, but thank heaven, this was turning out to be a minor mishap, not a major crisis.

"Did you stub your toe?" she asked, smoothing Kate's curls off her forehead. "On a rock?"

Kate nodded, her sniffles subsiding. "On a *big* rock," she said, indicating a small, bloodstained boulder. "It hurt me. Hi, Matt!" she added, lifting her foot and waving it in his direction. "Look at me! I'm all bloody."

He knelt beside her. "You sure are," he agreed. "Want to come with me, and I'll dip your feet in the water so's we can wash off the blood?"

Kate, still somewhat shocked by her accident, clung to Linda. "I want Mommy to come."

"Me, too!" Drew piped up. "I want to swim with Mommy."

Over the twins' heads, Matt glanced at Linda. "Do you want me to keep them amused while you get changed?"

"Thanks, if you would. I won't take a minute." She walked back to the picnic rug, heart pounding once again, but no longer from fright. She turned her back toward Matt and the twins and unbuckled her sandals, placing them neatly on a corner of the blanket. Beneath her shorts and shirt she wore a black, one-piece swimsuit. Her mother had approved the dark color and conservative cut, but Linda knew its modesty was deceiving. The plain style showed off every curve of her body, and the dull satiny sheen of the fabric emphasized her golden tan and the long length of her legs. In some ways, it was more tantalizing than a bikini.

She unfastened her blouse, her shaking fingers making slow work of the stiff buttons. It wasn't modesty or shyness that was making her so nervous, she admitted to herself. It was straightforward fear. Fear that Matt Deighton would no longer find her attractive. She could remember a time when a glimpse of her in a bikini had been enough to make his body taut with desire. Despite all that had happened in the years since, despite marriage to Jim and the pain of widowhood, she couldn't bear the thought that Matt should look at her now with any degree of indifference.

Linda stepped out of her shorts and turned around.

After seven years in New York City working on the fringes of a profession where women were willing to sleep with anybody who might have the power to give them a job, Matt thought he'd become immune to the impact of even the most beautiful female body. Linda showed him otherwise. He felt the tension build as she took off her shirt. By the time she discarded her shorts, he was remembering far too much that would have been better forgotten. The taste of her long-ago kisses was in his mouth, and he could recall each one of the forbidden places where he had touched her.

She turned around, and they stared at each other across the patch of grass. Dear God, but she had changed in the last seven years! At seventeen and a half, her body had held no more than the promise of woman-hood. At twenty-five, every promise had been fulfilled magnificently.

Matt's gaze raked over the swell of her breasts, the narrowness of her waist, the delicate flare of her hips, and the incredible, endless length of her legs. He smiled without mirth. The joke of it was, he couldn't risk looking at her for much longer. His mind might tell him that dozens of women in New York were more attractive, but his body was already hard with wanting.

Just like old times, he thought with a trace of self-mockery. He was going to have to dive into some cold water before he embarrassed the hell out of both of them. The situation was comic, but he felt more angry than amused. He was too damned old to be taking cold baths to cure his sexual arousal.

He took the twins by the hands, and walked across to meet Linda. "The twins would probably prefer to go in with you," he said curtly.

Her huge eyes darkened with something like pain. He dropped the children's hands and turned abruptly, running across the narrow strip of sandy shoreline. He made a flat racing dive into the shallows and struck out immediately for deeper waters.

The exercise helped less than it should have done, and his mood hovered somewhere between irritated and downright grouchy. He realized he was angry with Linda for being an unattainable, virtuous widow instead of an easy, amoral lay. Irrational, maybe, to blame Linda for his feelings, but he'd spent an entire summer burning up for her seven years ago, and he wasn't about to waste another two weeks of his life in a state of permanent frustration.

Matt reminded himself that there was a ready cure

for his problem. The doctor had sent him home to Colorado for rest and recreation. So far, all he'd done was rest. Tonight, for a change, he'd concentrate on recreation. He'd catch the evening flight from Grand Junction to Denver and see what that city had to offer in the way of feminine entertainment.

Matt concentrated his thoughts on lush female bodies encased in red satin underwear, lying on rumpled sheets. Oddly enough, this seemed to diminish his state of arousal sufficiently that he was able to swim back to the shallows and play with the twins. He was smart enough not to get too close to Linda. Red satin fantasies could protect him only so far.

He cut the afternoon short, claiming the need to get back to Carson as soon as they all emerged from the water. As he'd expected, Linda was too polite to ask what urgent business he had recalled. As a matter of fact, Linda had very little to say on the journey back to Carson, which was fortunate, because Matt certainly didn't feel in the mood to exchange idle chitchat. The twins slept most of the journey, and Linda appeared to be content to lean back in her seat and listen to country music on the radio.

About halfway home to Carson, Matt decided that returning home had sent his emotions back in a time warp. A few more hours in Linda's company, and he could visualize himself reverting to all the old, self-destructive patterns of behavior. But, Matt reminded himself grimly, he was seven years wiser than he had been when he first fell in love with innocent, vulnerable Lindy Beth Owen. This time he was going to think with his brains, not with his britches.

He had business to take care of in Denver, and a few days away from Carson was beginning to look more attractive by the minute. He would definitely leave to-night. And if the last scheduled flight had already left for the day, he'd charter his own airplane.

Life as a millionaire had its compensations.

Chapter Five

LINDA WAS VERY relieved when Drew and Kate settled themselves down for an afternoon nap on Tuesday with only token protests. She wanted to work on her Rumbles drawings, and the twins had reached the age where she could no longer count on a period of peace and quiet after lunch. Sometimes she thought that what she craved more than anything else in the world was an entire day to herself, without interruptions.

She closed the door of the twins' room and stepped softly into the upstairs hallway. Her heart sank clear into her neat white sandals when she saw her mother hunched on her knees scrubbing away at the paintwork outside the master bedroom.

Nora dipped her sponge into a pail of steaming, detergent-scented water. "Children settled?" she asked brightly, not pausing in her vigorous rubbing.

"Yes, thank goodness. I'm hoping they'll stay quiet for a couple of hours at least."

"It's always easier to work without the children underfoot," Nora agreed. "Do you need to get an apron? I brought up an extra sponge and a pair of rubber gloves. We'll have all these skirting boards gleaming before they wake up."

Guilt surged over Linda in a hot, thick wave.

"Mother, I'm sorry. I can't wash paint right now. I have something urgent to do while the twins are sleeping."

The scrubbing stopped for a split second, then resumed, faster than before. "You're going out?"

"No. I need to do some work on my Rumbles drawings. Somebody in New York wants to take a look at the whole series, and they're not ready. The concept sketches are okay, I think, but the patterns for the toys could be improved a lot."

Nora concentrated on wiping a finger plate, pushing the sponge deep into the grooves in the scrollwork. "My, this cleaning is hard work," she murmured, putting her hand to the small of her back and wincing ostentatiously. "Sometimes I wonder if I'm getting past it. Your dad and I aren't getting any younger, you know. He'll be sixty-three next birthday."

Linda gritted her teeth to stop herself apologizing. "Mother, we cleaned all this paintwork last month." She tried to joke. "You'll wash it away if you're not careful, and then Dad'll have to spend his summer vacation repainting."

"You can mock my cleaning habits if you want to, Lindy Beth, but I won't have dirt in my house. If you'd discipline the twins properly so that they didn't walk upstairs trailing their sticky hands along the wall—"

Linda felt her fingers curl themselves into two tight balls of tension. She thrust her hands behind her back, forcing herself to speak calmly. "I'll clean the walls tonight, Mother, once the twins are in bed, but I need to work on my drawings right now while the light's good."

Nora's lips tightened. "How did you hear tell of somebody in New York who's interested in seeing your drawings, anyway? I should think they've already got all the artists they need in that city. More than they need, for that matter. Why would anybody look at pictures drawn by an amateur from western Colorado, of all places?"

"Matt has a friend who's the president—"

Nora snorted. "I might have known it was something to do with That Man! Honestly, Lindy Beth, haven't you got more sense than to trust anything Matthew Deighton says! If he knows somebody who's a company president, why doesn't he get himself a job instead of stuffing your head full of nonsense?"

Nausea roiled violently through Linda's stomach. She'd always been hopeless at confrontations, especially when she wasn't at all sure she was in the right. Somehow, she had instinctively trusted Matt, but maybe she was naive to believe he had a friend who could help her. Maybe she was selfish to want these hours to herself. The twins made a lot of extra work for her parents, and she ought to be more considerate. After all, not many mothers of three-year-old twins had time to pursue their personal goals. And if she lived alone, in her own apartment, she would have all the housework to do, not just a share of it.

But if you lived alone, a rebellious voice pointed out, *you wouldn't waste your time and energy washing paintwork that already sparkles with cleanliness.* Her mother didn't clean house out of necessity, Linda found herself thinking. Nora cleaned house as her personal, all-consuming hobby. That was fine for Nora, but did Linda have to adopt the same obsession?

Linda's hand shook as she reached for the handle of her bedroom door, but she forced herself to meet Nora's accusing gaze. "Like I said, Mom, I'll scrub all the paint you want this evening, but right now, I'm planning to work on my Rumbles drawings."

Splotches of color mottled Nora's cheeks. "Well, I'm sure I don't know what Jim would have said—"

"Don't you?" Linda's smile contained no mirth at all. "He'd have said I ought to do whatever was right for me. He'd have meant it, too, even though he thought my drawings were a waste of time. Jim was unbearably tolerant of other people's weaknesses. That's just one of the reasons I found him such hell to live with."

Before Nora could gather her stunned wits sufficiently to comment, Linda slipped into her bedroom, shutting and locking the door behind her. Closing her eyes, she leaned for a moment against the hard panels of the door. This was the first time she had ever admitted to anybody that her married life hadn't been perfect, and she shook with reaction to her confession. When her knees finally stopped trembling, she walked determinedly over to her drafting table and selected a soft-lead pencil from the jar. With a ruthlessness she managed to exert only in relation to her work, she closed her mind to everything except the fantasy kingdom where the Rumbles lived.

No sounds from the house penetrated her concentration until a series of muffled squawks warned her that the twins were awake. Blinking, slightly disoriented, she came back into the everyday world—and immediately felt overwhelmed by guilt. She'd not only been inconsiderate of her mother's needs, she'd been downright rude into the bargain. What's more, her defiance probably served no useful purpose. As Nora had pointed out, Matt wasn't likely to know anybody influential, certainly not an executive with the power to make buying decisions for a major toy manufacturer. Resolving to apologize profusely to her mother for her bad behavior, Linda stuck her pencil back in the jar and hurried to the twins' room.

Nora was already there, helping the twins put on their socks. She looked up, her expression martyred. "If you're able to spare a few minutes to look after your children, Lindy Beth, I'll get back to the kitchen. I'm in the middle of peeling potatoes for tonight's dinner."

Linda silently counted to ten. "Sure, Mom. I planned to take the twins to the park to feed the ducks, and maybe swing on the swings in the playground. That is, if you don't have anything you want me to do."

"Oh, no, I daresay I'll manage on my own. I always do."

Linda counted to twenty. "We'll see you later then, Mom. Are you ready, kids?"

"We is thirsty," Kate said firmly.

"How about if I buy you a soda at Scoop-a-Doop?"

"Don't ruin their appetites for dinner," Nora warned over the squeals of excitement coming from the twins.

"No, Mother."

"By the way, if you're expecting to see That Man while you're out, you're going to be disappointed. He's in Denver, and Mrs. Wittmeyer says nobody knows when he'll be coming back."

Drew pulled his hand away from Linda's grasp. "Ouch, Mommy! You hurting!"

"Sorry, pet, I didn't mean to squeeze you." Linda put her son's hand to her mouth and gave it an absent-minded kiss. She looked up and threw her mother a challenging smile. "I didn't know Matt had left town, but when he gets back, I'm sure he'll want to see my drawings. Another two or three afternoons' work, and they'll be in pretty fair shape."

Nora straightened the cotton blanket on Kate's bed. "That Man always did play you for a fool, Lindy Beth."

"You know something, Mother? I'm not sure I give a damn."

Linda saw her mother's mouth fall open and marched out of the twins' room, feeling totally wonderful for all of thirty seconds. She stormed down the stairs, the twins tumbling alongside her. She was *tired* of being Little Miss Perfect, *tired* of always doing what other people wanted her to do. By the time she reached the foot of the stairs, her flair of anger dissipated, and she gave a rueful grimace. So much for abject apologies and keeping the peace! If she carried on the way she was going, the town of Carson was soon going to decide their resident angel had turned into the Wicked Witch of the West. But right at this moment, Wicked Witch was a role Linda found sinfully appealing.

Sally Deighton confirmed that her son had indeed disappeared into the fleshpots of Denver, but she didn't specify what he was doing there, and his activities remained a complete mystery to the curious folk of Carson. Even Mrs. Wittmeyer's jungle telegraph failed her. Much to her chagrin, she was unable to report any news of his doings. Jennifer Deighton remarked several times that he had business to attend to. Of course, nobody believed her, but nobody could actually disprove what she said, either.

After two or three days, the townsfolk gradually resigned themselves to the sad possibility that their favorite black sheep might not return to Carson. Their hopes for an entertaining new scandal gradually faded. Deprived of their preferred prey, they made as much as they could out of Jennifer's outrageous clothes and bizarre hairstyles, but even she failed to live up to expectations. She and her mother spent Wednesday and Thursday afternoon in Grand Junction shopping, but Mrs. Wittmeyer was compelled to report—very sadly—that Doug Hotchkiss had been nowhere in sight. Jennifer's mornings were spent even more tamely, relaxing with Linda and the twins in one or other of their backyards. Even the most ardent rumormongers could make nothing much out of such a harmless schedule.

For once, Linda wished that the town gossip mill could work a little more efficiently. She was dying to know what Matt's plans were, but years of accumulated inhibitions prevented her from asking outright. During their hours together, she and Jennifer seemed to touch upon every subject under the sun except the one Linda most wanted to discuss. Jennifer talked about her career, about the Rumbles, about the twins, about New York, about her brother Brian, who was a pilot with the air force in Germany, and about her sister-in-law, Brian's wife. Infuriatingly, Matt's name never crossed her lips. However hard Linda tried to edge the conversation around to the topic of where Matt was and when he might be coming back to Carson, Jennifer seemed to remain deaf to her hints.

Jennifer left for Denver on Friday morning, and Linda volunteered to drive her friend to the airport in Grand Junction. They left Carson soon after breakfast, the twins chattering excitedly, but Jennifer unusually silent.

Linda didn't force her friend to talk. The following Monday would be Jennifer's first day on the air as Channel 10's early-morning-news anchorwoman, so Linda wasn't altogether surprised to find the atmosphere inside the car somewhat tense. By the time they reached the airport parking lot, the tension inside the car had grown thick enough to cut with a knife. Even the twins had stopped their chattering and become unnaturally subdued.

Her friend's obvious nervousness began to worry Linda. There were sixty-odd hours left before the show went on the air. At this rate, Jennifer would be catatonic by the time the cameras started rolling.

"Don't worry, Jen," she said as they pulled into a parking space. "You'll be terrific, you know you will. After all, you have four years under your belt as a feature reporter. In comparison to the competition you faced in New York City, Denver's breakfast program ought to be a piece of cake."

"Yes, I guess so." Jennifer continued to stare out the window. A second or so later, she jerked her head around. "I'm sorry, Lindy, what did you say? My mind's wandering today."

"It wasn't important." Trying to change the subject to something Jennifer would find less nerve-wracking, Linda was delighted when she spotted a vaguely familiar figure on the other side of the parking lot.

"Oh, look, Jen! Isn't that Doug Hotchkiss? Good grief, he's certainly filled out since the last time I saw him. Do you think maybe he's taking the same flight into Denver you are?"

Jennifer jolted up in her set as if she'd been poked with an electric cattle prod. "He'd better be," she muttered under her breath. "I told him three times which one I'd be taking."

Linda observed in silent amazement as Doug Hotchkiss approached and her friend's cheeks grew steadily pinker. She was almost equally amazed by Jennifer's blushes and Doug's changed appearance. The former Nerd of the Year was dressed in immaculately tailored slacks and a crisp white shirt unbuttoned at the collar. He carried an expensive leather portfolio and a summer-weight jacket with a designer label slung over his shoulder. He was still slim, but otherwise he bore not the slightest resemblance to his weedy high school image.

"Hello, Doug," Linda said, smiling with real pleasure as she got out of the car to greet him. "What a nice surprise to see you again. Are you taking the Denver flight, too?"

"Hello, Lindy Beth, you're looking as gorgeous as ever. And these must be the twins I've heard so much about." Bending down, he shook hands solemnly. "Hi, kids, I'm very pleased to meet you."

"Hello," said Kate. "Who are you?"

"I'm an old friend of your mom's, and of Jennifer's. We're flying to Denver together."

"Not Mommy," Drew said quickly.

"No," Doug said reassuringly. "Not your mother. Just Jennifer and me."

Jennifer gave a strangled gasp. "I have to get my luggage," she said, grabbing the keys from Linda and making a dive for the back of the car. She opened the trunk and buried herself under the lid.

"Here, let me help you with that," Doug offered.

Jennifer shied away from his hands. "I'll be fine— *ouch!*"

Eyes watering, she leaned against the car, rubbing her head where she had banged it, and Doug swept her into his arms.

"Did you hurt yourself?" he asked anxiously, running long, sensitive fingers over the crown of her head. "You've got a bump there already. Why didn't you let me take care of your luggage?"

"I'm perfectly capable of taking care of it myself."

"Yes, I can see you are. That's why you nearly knocked yourself out reaching for your suitcase."

Instead of taking offense at this patronizing remark, Jennifer relapsed into silence. Linda watched in amusement as her sophisticated, world-weary friend gave every appearance of becoming hypnotized by one of Doug's shirt buttons. After a moment's speculative contemplation of the top of Jennifer's head, Doug muttered something to the effect of, "What have I got to lose?"

Clasping her firmly—with most un-nerdlike skill— he tipped her head back and kissed her with the fervor of a man finally in sight of heaven.

Drew and Kate watched this exhibition with interest. "Why don't they stop hugging and stuff?" Kate asked after some considerable time.

"Because they—um—like kissing each other, I suppose."

"Why?"

"I guess because they're in love."

"Why?"

Exasperated, Linda eyed her offspring. "It's difficult to explain why people fall in love," she said finally. "Look, I've had a great idea. Why don't we go and watch the planes come in to land? Jennifer and Doug will catch up with us later."

"They're asleep," Drew remarked. "Their eyes is shut tight." He tugged at Jennifer's pants. "Don't go to sleep, Jenny. Your plane is coming."

Jennifer and Doug sprang guiltily apart, both of them looking dazed. Linda held out her friend's leather briefcase. "You left this in the car," she said politely.

"Oh, thanks." Jennifer's attempt to sound nonchalant failed miserably, and Doug seemed to be entirely speechless.

Linda smothered a grin. If left to their own devices, she had no doubt they would both stand in the parking lot, staring into each other's eyes while their plane took off. The chemistry between the pair of them was so strong, she could almost feel the crackle.

"If you'll grab one of the suitcases, Doug, we could get you both checked in. Don't you have any luggage?"

He blinked, focusing his gaze on Linda with obvious

difficulty. "Luggage? Oh no, just my briefcase. I have an apartment in Denver. I keep a set of clothes there." He took the two suitcases out of the trunk, then stared at Jennifer as if unable to believe he was really seeing her.

"I've been wanting to kiss you like that since we were in high school," he said.

Some of Jennifer's natural tartness seemed to be returning. "Great," she said, as they trooped into the terminal building. "Is it going to take another eight years before you work out what happens next?"

Doug flashed her a smile. "Don't worry, darling. Some things I can work out much faster than in the old days. How about coming to my apartment for dinner tonight?"

Jennifer scowled, obviously trying to rebuild her usual shell of flip sophistication. "I suppose whipping up gourmet meals is another one of the skills you've acquired since I left town."

"No, but I'm a whiz at dialing the caterers." He put down the cases in front of the airline counter and took her hands into his. Linda could actually see the trembling response that quivered through her friend. "What do you say, Jen? May I pick you up at seven?"

Jennifer stared down at their intertwined hands. Color flared along her cheekbones, and for a moment she looked very beautiful. "Seven sounds good," she murmured.

Doug's breath expelled in a long sigh. Linda decided he hadn't been quite as confident of the outcome of his invitation as he'd appeared. "If you give me your ticket, I'll check us in," was all he said. "Follow me through to the gate when you're ready."

He said good-bye to Linda and the twins, then presented the tickets to the airline clerk.

Jennifer turned her back on him and gave each of the

twins a hug, studiously avoiding Linda's gaze. She extracted two lollipops from her trouser pocket, feigning bewilderment as she held them out to the twins. "Well, how in the world did these get into my pockets? I'm not the least bit hungry right now. Would you two like to help me out by eating them?"

The twins expressed suitable willingness, and Jennifer handed over the candy. Then she thrust her hands into her pockets, her stance aggressive as she finally faced Linda. "You don't have to tell me we're not suited," she said gruffly. "I know that."

Linda thought of Jim, dear, kind Jim who had been such an eminently "suitable" husband for her—except that she hadn't loved him. "How do you tell when people are suited to each other?" she asked. "You practically ignited when Doug was kissing you. That has to mean something."

"Yeah. It means we turn each other on. Big deal."

"Aren't you the person who told me a couple of days ago that *good* sex is the answer to every woman's problems?"

"There's more to a relationship than sex, even good sex." Jennifer pulled a comic face. "Damn! I don't believe I said that. Isn't that supposed to be your line?"

"Not mine," Linda said quietly. "Unless you can set each other on fire in the bedroom, I don't think a long-term relationship ever has a chance."

Jennifer looked at her friend intently. "Matt's flying home tomorrow," she said with seeming inconsequence. "As far as I know, he doesn't have any plans for the evening."

Linda became very absorbed in wiping Drew's sticky fingers. "Matt and I . . . there's too much baggage from the past, Jen. It would never work."

"Have you given it a try?" Jennifer didn't wait for an

answer. She turned abruptly. "I must go. They're calling my flight. Watch the show on Monday and tell me I'm terrific, even if it's a lie."

"What else are friends for? Besides, you will be terrific, so I won't need to lie."

Jennifer slung her purse over her shoulder. "Matt's plane gets in at four o'clock," she said, and walked off toward the gate without a backward glance.

Ron and Nora Owen left for their usual Saturday-night bowling game promptly at six o'clock. The twins, exhausted after an afternoon spent playing with friends, fell asleep at seven in the middle of listening to Linda read them a bedtime story. Which only partially explained why, at seven-fifteen, Linda was pacing the floor of the kitchen, arguing with herself, and losing both sides.

She made it twice to the telephone, but each time she hung up without dialing. On her third attempt, she snatched the receiver from its hook, as if afraid it might bite. She paced up and down the kitchen a few more times, then finally punched out the Deightons' number with shaking fingers. Even so, she would probably have hung up if the phone hadn't been answered on the first ring.

"Hello."

It was crazy that his voice could have such a startling effect on her. Crazy that her heart was pounding and her mouth dry just because he'd answered the phone. She swallowed to moisten her parched throat.

"Hi, Matt. This is Linda. I've just finished fixing dinner for myself, and I wondered if you'd like to come over and share it with me. I made way too much for one person."

There was a tiny pause. "Sounds great. Thanks. What have you cooked?"

"Cooked?" she repeated numbly. "Cooked?" She stared around the kitchen, with its bare, gleaming counters and empty stove. Good grief, she had the conspiratorial powers of the average first-grader! "Lasagna," she said frantically. "Yes, that's it. I've cooked lasagna."

"Terrific, I'm a sucker for Italian food. I'll see what Ben's liquor store has to offer and bring some wine. Fifteen minutes okay?"

"Fifteen minutes?" Linda almost shrieked into the phone. How in the world was she to cook lasagna in fifteen minutes? What was wrong with her tonight anyway? Had she totally lost her senses? Maybe she could order pizza and he wouldn't notice the difference. At least pizza was Italian.

"Give me half an hour," she said, wondering how she managed to sound so calm.

"I'm already working up an appetite."

He hung up the phone and she wasted at least two of her precious thirty minutes staring blankly at the receiver, listening to the dial tone. Then she shot off the stool and tore into the garage, muttering prayers she knew she didn't deserve to have answered.

On the middle shelf of the freezer she found a Pyrex baking dish, wrapped in several layers of plastic wrap and labeled *lasagna* in her mother's neat, round script. Linda seized it with eager hands. "Thank you, God," she breathed. "I owe you one."

She turned the regular oven onto preheat, put the casserole dish into the microwave to defrost for twenty minutes, then ran to the fridge and assembled the makings of a salad. After five minutes of top-speed chopping and shredding, she scattered a handful of scallions

over the rest of the ingredients and shoved the glass
bowl into the fridge. Rinsing her hands under the cold
tap, she reflected with wry humor that this was one
salad that could well and truly be called tossed.

The stark white of Nora Owen's kitchen wasn't con-
ducive to cozy meals, so she laid two places in the dining room, drawing the drapes and lighting candles with
a touch of bravado. Fortunately, there wasn't time to
analyze her motives in setting such a flagrantly romantic
scene.

The kitchen was already beginning to smell appetiz-
ingly of oregano and mozzarella when the timer on the
microwave beeped. Ten minutes in the regular oven
should do it, she thought, placing the dish of lasagna on
the middle shelf and adjusting the thermostat.

She had five minutes left to do something about her
appearance. She dashed up to her room to apply some
lipstick and stared into the mirror, amazed to find that
her reflection looked pretty much the same as always.
Her blue eyes revealed nothing of her frazzled inner
state, and her upswept blond hair remained smoothly
confined in a French twist. As for her short-sleeved shirt
and tailored slacks, they both looked immaculate.

Oddly dissatisfied with her chaste appearance, Linda
unfastened the top button of her blouse. She still looked
like somebody auditioning to play the part of Grace
Kelly. Scowling, she undid another button, then in a fit
of recklessness pulled all the pins out of her hair. Released from bondage, her hair tumbled in a heavy mass
of loose curls about her shoulders.

The front doorbell rang, restoring her sanity in a
cold, hard flash. Good heavens, she couldn't possibly
answer the door to Matthew Deighton looking like this!
Her clumsy fingers refused to cooperate as she tried to
twist her hair back into its usual style. The doorbell rang

again, and with a despairing sigh, she gave up on the French twist, cramming as much of her hair as possible into a barrette fastened at the nape of her neck. She ran down the stairs and opened the door.

Matt, wearing his inevitable jeans and casual knit shirt, waited on the top step, holding a bottle of wine. He looked—darn him!—sexy enough to set Linda's, and any other woman's, knees knocking. He didn't say anything, just looked at her with those laughing blue eyes that she could have sworn had the power to physically stroke her. Her skin heated everywhere his gaze touched, melting her common sense, coaxing back memories of that summer when she had first begun to learn the meaning of passion.

"May I come in?" Matt asked, smiling softly. "My spine's beginning to give off warning tingles. One of Mrs. Wittmeyer's investigators must be on the prowl."

"Oh, yes, I'm sorry," Linda said. "Come into the kitchen, and you can open the wine while I put the dressing on the salad."

He followed her down the hall, sniffing appreciatively. "You realize that by tomorrow morning, Mrs. Wittmeyer will be telling everybody how we bedded down on the living room sofa for a night of wild, orgiastic sex. Does that bother you?"

"Some. A lot less than it would have in the past. How about you?"

Matt grinned. "Sure it bothers me. Not because she'll tell everybody we indulged in a night of wild sex, but because it won't be true."

Linda bit her lip to hide a smile. "You're getting staid and respectable, Matt. In the old days, you'd have made sure you lived up to any stories Mrs. Wittmeyer could invent."

His eyes gleamed. "Sweetheart, I'm game if you are."

"Open the wine, Matt," she said, her voice dry.

"I brought a corkscrew," he said, pulling it from his back pocket. He leaned against the counter, his mere presence making the sterile atmosphere of the kitchen warmer and less antiseptic. "I didn't know if your parents would have one."

"Oh, yes, they're not teetotalers. Why don't you take the wine through to the dining room, and I'll bring in the food."

The lasagna seemed to have survived its brutal reheating, a profound tribute to Nora's culinary skills. Matt's red Burgundy made the perfect accompaniment, slipping smoothly over Linda's tongue. She relaxed as she listened to Matt's colorful stories about his early days in Manhattan, laughing softly when he told some particularly outrageous tale. This is how it ought to be, she thought drowsily. Old friends sharing a good meal, catching up on each other's news, feeling *comfortable* together.

"I'm glad you came back to Carson, Matt," she said.

"Are you?" He leaned back in his chair, sipping his wine. "I called my friend in New York a couple of days ago. He says he'd be interested in seeing your Rumbles drawings if I think they look promising."

Linda had drunk three glasses of wine, two-and-a-half glasses more than her normal allowance. Her courage increased proportionately. "My Rumbles drawings aren't promising, they're spectacular," she said with more than a touch of belligerence. "Do you want to see them? I've been working on them all week."

"Maybe we should take the dishes into the kitchen first."

"Let's not. Unfortunately, they won't disappear if we

leave them." She waved her hand vaguely over the table. "I'll clear up after you've gone home. Want to come upstairs to my bedroom?"

Matt glanced wryly from the wine bottle to Linda. "Is that where you keep the Rumbles drawings?"

"Of course, what else?"

"What else indeed," he murmured, pulling back his chair. "Can you make it upstairs?"

"Why ever not?" she asked, affronted.

"Oh, I had this crazy idea you might not be used to drinking so much wine."

"I'm twenty-five," Linda said with great dignity. "I *often* drink wine. And beer, too," she added as an afterthought.

"Mmm. Twice a year at least."

"Hah! Much more often," she said, flicking on the overhead light in her bedroom. "Probably once a month." She turned on the special fluorescent strip over her drafting table. "If you sit here, you'll be able to see better. I'll get the drawings."

He caught her wrist as she walked by. "Linda, you realize my friend is relying on me to make a business judgment. You know I'll have to tell you the truth if I don't think your drawings are commercially up to the mark?"

The delightful floating effect of the alcohol dissipated in an instant. "I wouldn't want it any other way," she said.

"If you're sure. Sometimes people prefer to hang on to their dreams."

"Not me. I'm a realist." Linda spoke the words bravely enough, but she wasn't sure she told the truth. In creating the Rumbles, she'd allowed herself to express all the emotions she repressed in everyday life. Several of the Rumbles had personalities based on years of observing human nature in a small town. Her two favorites, the Baby Rumbles, were loving caricatures of Drew and Kate. If Matt decided the drawings were terrible, he might destroy something she had taken years to create. Wouldn't it be better to protect her dreams? she wondered. Even if it meant the Rumbles could never be more for her than an absorbing hobby?

Like your mother's housecleaning. The insidious thought flashed unbidden into Linda's mind. Did she want her drawings to become an addictive pastime that enabled her to avoid dealing with real people and real situations? Her own past experiences should have taught her by now that if dreams weren't put to the test, they rapidly turned into nightmares.

With shaking fingers, she removed her portfolio of drawings from the closet. "Here," she said, putting the folder in front of Matt. She plunked herself down on the bed, unable to bear the tension of watching him.

He opened the portfolio and stared at the first forest scene for a long time before turning to the next page. He made no sound at all, not even a grunt of approval or a sigh of displeasure. Linda's eyes bored into his back. Never in her whole entire life had she seen such an uncommunicative human body. Slowly, he turned over several more pages. Linda clasped her hands in her lap and stared at her fingers as if she had never seen them before. She had long, slender thumbs and square fingernails, she noted absently. What an odd combination.

Matt turned the last two pages. He closed the folder and gazed silently ahead of him. Linda sprang to her feet and rushed over to grab her drawings. Better not to let him speak.

"Look, Matt, I'm sober now, so you don't have to be nice. I realize I'm just an amateur, and I understand why Playbrite can't use these—"

"They're brilliant," Matt said quietly. "My mother told me they were, but I didn't believe her. Your patterns look to me as if they still need some simplification, but your concept drawings are stunning. Your technique is sophisticated, and your ideas are totally original. My com... My friend's company had better snap you up fast, or Mattel and Coleco are going to be fighting over you."

Linda stared down at her drawings. "They're good?" she asked, her voice cracking. "You really think your friend might buy them?"

"I'm certain he will. I'll send some samples of your work to New York by Federal Express. He could arrange to have the company lawyer in Denver by Wednesday. How do you feel about signing a licensing agreement? They'd make it very fair. They'd pay you a royalty, so you'd make money on every Rumble that was sold."

Linda sat down again on her bed, scarcely able to absorb what Matt was saying. "I think I need another glass of wine."

He grinned. "Sorry, sweetheart, but you already drank it all."

Linda shook her head, trying to restore a sense of reality. "I'm building too many fantasies on your reaction, Matt. After all, even though you like the drawings, that doesn't mean your friend will. What's his name, by the way?"

"Charlie. And I assure you Charlie will take my advice in this. You have my promise."

Linda was too dazed by wine and happiness to analyze his words carefully. She jumped up and flung her arms around Matt's neck. "Thank you," she whispered. "You can't even begin to guess what this means to me. Thank you for everything."

Matt stood still, his face expressionless as he gazed down at her. "What does it mean to you, Linda?"

"Independence." She said the word reverently. "The chance to have my own apartment, to make my own decisions—" She broke off abruptly, afraid to sound disloyal to her parents after all they'd done for her when Jim died.

His arms tightened for a moment around her waist. "Sounds pretty exciting. I'm glad I could help."

"It is exciting." She smiled up at him, and he gazed back, his eyes containing no hint of their usual laughter. She suddenly felt giddy again, although she knew that the cause this time had nothing to do with Burgundy wine. She took a deep breath and swayed forward, allowing her body to curve against Matt's.

His hand touched her face. "Linda, are you all right?"

She took another breath. "Yes."

His hand lingered on her cheek, and without giving herself time for conscious thought, she turned her head and fleetingly pressed her lips against his palm.

She felt his whole body grow taut. "Linda?" he said huskily, his voice rising in an unspoken question.

"I'm sorry," she whispered. "I didn't mean—" She tore herself out of his embrace, shocked by her own earlier action and by the immediate response she had felt in his body.

"I'm not," he said softly, and drew her back into his arms. He cupped her face with shaking fingers, and bent his head until his mouth touched hers.

For a moment, there was nothing more than the butterfly touch of his lips against her mouth. Then seven years of emptiness fell away in an instant, and Linda reached out to pull him closer, her fingers losing themselves in the springy thickness of his hair. "Hold me," she murmured. "Oh, Matt, please hold me."

His kiss was hungry, passionate, and yet incredibly tender. She opened her mouth, yearning for the taste of him, for the caress of his tongue moving inside her mouth. She wanted to draw him into her body, to absorb him, to feel the universe explode around her in the way only he could make happen. Heat surged through her chest, and her hips rocked toward him. She felt the hardness of his erection against her stomach, and her body responded with an involuntary leap of nervous excitement.

Neither of them spoke. It was as if words would break the spell of their lovemaking, forcing them to look logically at a situation they both preferred to leave unexamined. Their kiss became almost savage, their lips biting against each other, his tongue thrusting deep inside her mouth, demanding submission. When his hands slipped inside her shirt, Linda didn't resist, arching herself against him even before his fingers curved around her throbbing breasts. She shivered with pleasure when his callused thumbs rasped across her nipples.

Outside, darkness had long since fallen, and the pounding rains of a summer thunderstorm cooled the air of her bedroom. She didn't notice the chill, because a hot tide of desire had invaded her body, flushing her skin and firing her blood. Her breath came hard and uneven, and the blood thrummed in her ears, deafening her to the boom of thunder and the splash of rain. She was barely conscious of Matt's hands unbuttoning her blouse. Her world centered on the caress of his fingers against her breasts, and the touch of his lips as they moved against her mouth, drawing her into him, making them one.

"Oh, dear heavens, Lindy Beth! What's going on in here?"

For a split second, she didn't register the sound of her mother's voice. When Matt suddenly wrenched his mouth away, she moaned, closing her eyes and turning blindly to seek him again.

"Lindy Beth! How could you? Bringing that dreadful man up to your bedroom with those poor innocent children in the house and the dinner dishes still on the table!"

Matt continued to hold her, which was fortunate, because Linda wasn't at all sure she could have stood unsupported. He kept her back turned toward the door and quietly refastened the buttons on her blouse. "You look fine now," he murmured, dropping a light kiss on the end of her nose. "You can turn around, if you want."

She blinked, trying desperately to orient herself. Frustration gnawed at her powers of concentration. Physical frustration, because her body still cried out for Matt's lovemaking. Mental frustration, because she realized there was something very wrong with her relationship with her parents for this situation to have arisen.

"Lindy Beth!" Her mother's exclamation hammered at her ears, making rational thought impossible. "Lindy Beth, I asked for an explanation. I *demand* an explanation."

Linda looked up at Matt, instinctively seeking his help. Incredibly, unbelievably, she saw him smile.

"Sorry about the dishes, Mrs. Owen," he said easily. "If we'd known you'd be home this early, we'd have washed up sooner."

Chapter Six

NORA'S NOSTRILS FLARED with temper. "You know perfectly well, Matthew Deighton, that I wasn't asking why the dinner dishes are still on the table."

"Then what did you want explained, Mrs. Owen?" Matt's manner was polite, but the thread of steel running through his words was unmistakable, at least to Linda.

"Don't try to get clever with me, Matt! You know very well what I mean. What were you and my daughter doing in her bedroom when I came up here?"

"We were kissing," Matt explained politely.

Nora's cheeks puffed out so far, she appeared on the verge of apoplexy. "Kissing, indeed! People never kissed like that in my day."

Matt clucked sympathetically. "Gee, I'm really sorry."

"I'm telling you straight, Matthew Deighton, I won't have such immoral goings-on in my house!"

Nora was sputtering with anger, and Linda automatically sought to play her usual role of peacemaker. "Mom, please, don't get all worked up about nothing. You know you won't be able to sleep tonight if you get yourself upset."

"I'm already upset!"

Matt straightened, his indolent good humor dropping

away when it became clear that Nora couldn't be teased into reasonableness. "And I'm telling *you* straight, Mrs. Owen, that Linda is twenty-five years old and single. She's an adult, free to make her own choices, even if you don't approve. Just because something's pleasurable, you know, doesn't make it immoral."

"Maybe not. Maybe kissing's nothing to make a fuss about. But it's what you'd have been doing to our poor Lindy Beth if we hadn't gotten home early that I worry about!"

"Doing to her?" Matt repeated, his mouth curling in distaste. "Whatever might have happened in this bedroom if you hadn't burst into it, Mrs. Owen, you can rest assured Linda would have been my partner, not my victim."

Tears filled Nora's eyes, and her voice rose hysterically. "She doesn't want to have anything to do with you! You're all wrong for my little girl, and you always will be!"

"Mom, please don't upset yourself any more." Linda couldn't bear to see her mother so distraught. Intellectually, she realized that Nora's behavior was ridiculous, but she was conditioned by a lifetime of wanting to please, and in her parents' home she felt an obligation to behave according to their rules. She looked at Matt, hoping against hope that he would understand why she chose to placate her mother. Of course he didn't. She shivered when his gaze flicked over her, laced with scorn.

It was the same old story, Linda thought wanly. Matt had never understood her deeply rooted sense of obligation toward her parents. Whereas she, unfortunately, had never been able to forget all that she owed them. Her parents had waited fourteen years to have a baby, and she understood that even their most aggravating actions were motivated by love. If only the intensity of their love hadn't forged shackles Linda could find no will to resist!

"Mom, you're worrying needlessly," she said, touching Nora's arm in a soothing gesture. "Nothing would have happened here tonight whatever time you came back. Nothing at all."

"I thought a couple of things had already happened," Matt said with dangerous calm.

Nora's eyes darted from her daughter to Matt and back again. Her hand crept to her throat. "Wh-what does he mean, Lindy Beth?"

Linda damped down the urge to tell her mother to stop acting like a bad actress in a Victorian melodrama. "He doesn't mean anything very dreadful, do you, Matt?"

He looked at her long and hard. "No," he said finally. "Nothing dreadful."

"I invited Matt over for dinner, and then he offered to look at my Rumbles drawings," Linda explained. "He thinks his friend who's the president of Playbrite will want to license them for his toy company. Isn't that wonderful news?"

"Isn't what wonderful?" Ron Owen inquired, poking his head around the door. "And what's everybody doing up here in Lindy's bedroom, if that isn't a rude question?"

Matt strolled over to the drafting table and picked up Linda's portfolio. "Your daughter brought me upstairs to show me the drawings and toy patterns she's been working on, Ron. I'm planning to send some samples of her work to New York, and I hope that by Wednesday the toy company can get a lawyer out here to discuss licensing arrangements with Linda. Unfortunately, I suspect it's too late for Playbrite to gear up for this year's

Christmas production, but by next Christmas I'll bet half the kids in America will be asking Santa for a Rumbles toy. In my opinion, Linda's exceptionally talented."

Ron looked more worried than excited. "Well, that's wonderful news in some ways, Matt, and of course Lindy Beth could sure use the extra money. But would she have to live in New York? There are the twins to think of, and a big city like that would be a terrible place to bring up young children."

"New York?" Nora gasped, her face a picture of horror as she registered this new threat. "Oh, Lindy Beth, surely you wouldn't take the children away from us? Whatever would your dad and I do?" She corrected herself hastily. "I mean, you wouldn't take the twins away from a nice safe town like Carson to live in *New York?*"

Nora spat out the last two words as if she were discussing the darkest circle of Dante's hell, and a knife-blade of anger began to cut through the tangle of Linda's other emotions. "I expect I'd have to visit New York," she said curtly. "Matt and I haven't talked about how much input the toy company would need from me. That's not something he could possibly know."

Nora looked at the stubborn tilt of her daughter's chin and deployed her ultimate weapon. She burst into tears. "I can't believe you're going through with this crazy scheme, Lindy Beth. You don't really need the money. Your dad and I offer you a comfortable home—"

Linda took hold of her erupting temper and forced herself to speak calmly. "Mom, the twins are growing up. We're soon going to need an apartment of our own, and I can't afford even a one-bedroom walk-up on Jim's insurance. Some time soon I'll have to get a job. If I can support the twins by my artwork, isn't that much better for everybody?"

Nora choked back a dramatic sob. "We took you back into our home when you were desperate for a place to go. After all your father and I have done for you, this is the thanks we get. At the first opportunity, you turn your back on us."

Ron patted his wife's shoulder awkwardly, obviously embarrassed by her outburst, but incapable of handling it despite forty years of experience. "There, there, dear. Nothing's decided yet. Don't take on so. Why don't you come down to the kitchen, and we'll have some iced tea?"

Linda reached out to her mother. "Mom, I'm sorry. If it's all that important to you, I won't go."

Matt grabbed her arm, dragging her back toward the windows. His blue eyes blazed almost black with suppressed anger. "Linda, don't say it, please. For godsake, don't apologize to your mother because you're talented and hardworking and want to make something of your life."

Linda listened to the snuffle of Nora's sobs retreating down the stairs. "They only want what's best for me and the twins."

"They don't understand you well enough to decide what's best for you. Dammit, they've never even *tried* to understand you."

"They want to protect me from being hurt."

"Cocoons make first-rate prisons, have you ever thought about that, Linda?" He released her and ran his hand distractedly through his hair. "What the hell! It's none of my business. Walk me to the front door, will you?"

On the porch, he took her hands and raised them to his lips in a courtly gesture that ought to have seemed out of place but didn't. "Don't give in to them, whatever emotional blackmail they use, Linda. Your family of Rumbles deserve to see the light of day. Fly into Denver with me on Wednesday morning, and we'll meet with the lawyer. You have exceptional artistic talent, and you owe it to yourself to develop that talent commercially."

Too much had happened in one short evening, and she couldn't cope mentally with the wider implications of his words. Instead, she concentrated on the practical difficulties of her immediate situation. "My mother may refuse to baby-sit for the twins," she said.

"Tell her *my* mother would be delighted to look after them if she's too busy." Matt's voice was acid. "That should do the trick."

Linda's smile was rueful. "Yes, I'm sure it will."

"Your parents'll need to know when we'll be back. Tell them we'll catch the afternoon flight on Thursday."

"You mean we'll have to stay in Denver overnight?"

"There may be loose ends to tie up," Matt said vaguely. "Calls back and forth to New York. Negotiating the terms of a contract isn't that easy." He ruffled her hair in a casual gesture of farewell. "Take care, Linda. I'll be over to pick you up at seven o'clock on Wednesday morning."

Right up until the last minute, Matt expected Linda to produce some excuse as to why she couldn't accompany him to Denver. She surprised him by being ready right on time. He halted the car outside her parents' driveway, but before he could get out and ring the doorbell, she emerged from the house, carrying a small overnight case.

She wore a silky dark blue dress and matching high-heeled sandals. With her blond hair swept back into its usual neat style, she looked cool, businesslike, and much more fashionable than he'd anticipated. He should have realized, of course, that anybody with an artist's eye as acute as Linda's would have an instinct for fashion. Like the stunning swimsuit she'd worn to Benton Reservoir, this dress looked demure but actually carried a potent sexual punch. Although, Matt reflected wryly, the punch could have a lot to do with the body inside the dress. He'd always considered himself a dedicated leg man where females were concerned, but you didn't need to suffer from a breast fetish to find yourself fantasizing about the delectable curves that shaped the silk above Linda's narrow waist and flat stomach.

Soon, he promised himself. Soon he would turn fantasy into reality. Tonight he would take Linda to his bed and finally put his seven-year-old ghosts to rest. In another week, he'd be leaving Carson, and this time he didn't intend to carry away with him any regrets or frustrations.

As for how Linda might be affected by a one-night stand . . . well, he didn't intend to hurt her. Once upon a time, her nature had been deeply passionate. Carson and her parents had made her so repressed he was sure a few hours of sexual fun and games would be positively good for her. Therapeutic. Sort of like vitamins, only better. After nearly three years of chaste widowhood, Linda must need sex, and she would benefit greatly from finding a friendly partner to fulfill her physical needs. There would be no danger of emotional wounds for either of them. The passions of their old romance had long since died. Now they were just friends with a lingering, not-too-important attraction for each other's bodies. They no longer cared enough to be capable of inflicting emotional pain.

Glossing over the inconsistencies in his train of thought, Matt managed to ignore an uneasy tug at the edges of his conscience. He smiled easily as he opened the car door for Linda. "Hi! No problems getting away?"

"No problems," she said, putting her case onto the back seat of the car. "I left the twins eating breakfast."

"Nora doesn't mind baby-sitting?"

Linda grimaced. "Let's just say your ploy worked well. Mom would baby-sit for a month rather than allow your mother to have charge of the twins for five minutes."

He grinned. "Tut, tut, Linda, could it be that Carson's resident angel used calculated manipulation to get her own way? Your halo's slipping, honey."

She pulled a face as he eased behind the wheel. "I've no halo left to slip. As far as the townsfolk are concerned, it fell off in one fell swoop the day I accepted your invitation to picnic at the reservoir."

"Head feeling the chill, Lindy Beth?"

She looked at him steadily. "No. Just feeling a lot less burdened."

Matt backed off from the intimacy he could feel growing between the two of them. He wanted Linda's designs for the Rumbles to have the success they deserved, and he wanted to make love to her, but he wasn't about to get emotionally involved with a small-town girl whose lifestyle and values were the antithesis of his own. He changed the emotional temperature by asking about the twins. "This is the first time you've left Drew and Kate overnight, isn't it? Are you worried?"

"I am, but I know I shouldn't be."

"They're in familiar surroundings, with two people they love—"

"It's me I'm worried about, not the twins," she admitted ruefully. "I'm scared to death they won't miss me."

"There's no danger of that, I'm sure."

"Huh, that's how much you know about children, Matt Deighton. Enough ice-cream cones from my dad, and they won't even notice I'm gone."

"I see your problem. At this time of year, ice cream is tough competition."

"Sure is." She leaned forward, her smile turning to a frown. "Matt, there's something we have to talk about. These past two days, there never seemed to be a chance to discuss anything privately."

He could have pointed out that there would have been plenty of opportunities for private conversation if Nora Owen had possessed even a grain of tact, but right at this moment he had no interest in rubbing salt into old wounds. Quite apart from his determination to bed Linda and get her out of his system once and for all, he genuinely wanted her to enjoy the trip. "Discuss away," he said. "What's the problem?"

"It's about money, Matt." She unzipped her purse and pulled out a bank book. "I have a check already made out to you, to reimburse you for the cost of the plane tickets." She cleared her throat. "Both tickets, Matt. If you'll just tell me the amount, I'll fill it in."

For a split second, he debated telling her that he had enough money to buy the plane, let alone a couple of tickets, but something—pride perhaps—held him back. "There's no need," he said gruffly. "Linda, I can afford to pay for the tickets, I promise you."

"But I know you're between jobs, Matt." She looked at him earnestly, her cheeks flushed with embarrassment as she pressed her point. "If it weren't for you, I'd have had no idea where to take the Rumbles, or how to set about getting my designs sold. The least I can do is cover the costs of this trip, and that includes our rooms at the hotel. New York City's expensive, Matt. If you don't get that construction job you were hoping for, you may need this check for rent money."

"The construction job?" he repeated.

"Yes, you know. The job your dad mentioned when the twins and I came over to your house for dinner."

Enlightenment dawned. "Oh, that," he said. "Actually, that project came through for me, I heard a couple of days ago. So you see, you don't have to worry, Linda, I'm gainfully employed."

Her eyes sparkled. "For the whole summer?"

"Longer. And I'm hired on as what you might call project manager. I don't know who's going to be more amazed by my success, you or Mrs. Wittmeyer."

"Oh, Matt, that's wonderful! Project manager—I'm so pleased for you."

Linda turned to him, her whole face glowing, too happy to hear the thread of sarcasm running through his words. "I still want this trip to be my treat," she said. "Now we have two things to celebrate, your new job and mine! Oh, Matt, I think we're going to have fun, don't you? It's *ages* since I was in Denver. I'm going to order lobster for dinner tonight, unless there's something more expensive on the menu. I feel in the mood to splurge."

He couldn't have explained, even to himself, why he didn't cut through the morass of misunderstandings by telling her that the construction job he'd just landed wasn't anything like what she was thinking, that he hadn't been unemployed, that he wasn't poor. That he was, in fact, successful beyond her wildest imaginings.

Matt's hands tightened on the steering wheel. The words of confession formed on his lips, then died away unspoken. He allowed his eyes to rest on Linda's face, not attempting to hide the odd mixture of tenderness and sexual desire he felt. "I think this trip's going to be fun, too," he said softly.

The pink in her cheeks turned to the dusky red of awareness, and he retreated behind a more businesslike manner. He had all night to fan the flames of her desire, and he suspected it would be a mistake to come on too strong too soon.

"The plane tickets cost a hundred fifty dollars each," he said briskly. "It sounds like a lot, but unfortunately you can't get any bargains on these short, in-state hops."

She gulped, then wrote in the total with a flourish. "I can afford more than three hundred dollars now that I'm rich and famous," she said, and chuckled. "At least, I can afford it if Playbrite doesn't take forever to make their first royalty payment."

"My God, Linda, you have to ask for an up-front advance! You don't sell designs like yours without getting a down payment on the contract!"

"You mean Playbrite makes me a loan or something?"

"No!" He swallowed an exasperated expletive. "Not a loan, Linda. I mean an up-front cash payment to cement the deal. From the conversation I've had with Charlie, I'm sure he plans to offer you a decent advance. But if the lawyer hasn't written anything into the provisional contract, ask for it. You have to assert all your claims now, Linda, while they're still persuading you to sign. Once you've put your name on the dotted line, Playbrite sure isn't going to improve the terms of its offer."

"Oh," Linda said again. She was silent for a minute, obviously thinking about his advice. "Have you any idea how much of an advance I should ask for? Would a thousand dollars be too much?"

Matt frowned. He was fast walking himself right into the middle of a difficult situation. As a director of Playbrite, his responsibility was to protect the company and its profitability. As Linda's friend, he had a responsibility to see she made the best deal possible. Either way, he ought to tell her what his association with the company actually was.

But he didn't. Partly he supposed his silence was caused by pique. In his heart of hearts, Matt resented Linda's blithe assumption that he'd failed in his chosen career. It was one thing for Mrs. Wittmeyer to assume he'd spent the past seven years being a failure in New York City. It was another thing for Linda to reach the same unfounded conclusions. And partly he supposed he remained silent because he didn't want to bring too much of the real world into the bubble of naive excitement she was creating around them. For once, he wanted to have a relationship with a woman where he was just Matt. He was tired of being Grant Deighton, the man *Time* magazine had described as "the most innovative and most successful set designer at work today." Too often over the past year he'd found himself wondering whether the women in his bed were making love to him or to his reputation. When he finally held Linda in his arms again, he wanted to be absolutely confident of why she was there.

"I think Playbrite might go for ten thousand," he said finally.

There was a stunned silence. "Ten thousand dollars?" Linda whispered.

"If the Rumbles are successful, Playbrite will eventually make several million. I think they can spring for ten thousand without too much trouble."

"If the company makes several million..." Linda didn't manage to get the words out. She swallowed and tried again. "If Playbrite makes several million, how much will I make in royalties?" she asked in a small voice.

"A couple hundred thousand at least."

"Two hundred thousand dollars!"

"If that doesn't seem like a fair division of the profits, you have to remember all the development expenses Playbrite—"

"Shh," she said, leaning back in the seat and closing her eyes. "Matt, don't speak. I don't want to be bothered with facts and figures. I'm indulging in a Cinderella fantasy, and you're interrupting my delightful train of thought."

He smiled, waiting for a second or two before he spoke. "Who's your Prince Charming?"

"Who knows? Who cares?" She opened her eyes and glanced at him teasingly. "My imagination hasn't stretched to boring details like that. It's still working on the designer dress, the Tiffany jewels, and the horseless carriage. I thought maybe a black Porsche. What do you think?"

"I think that poor old Prince Charming is a lot less important in the Cinderella story than we men want to believe."

Linda's expression sobered. "He's important," she said. "The wrong prince ruins everything."

Knowing Linda, Matt had planned his strategy carefully. He warned her only moments before they arrived at the Westin Hotel that he'd booked just one room for the night. "It has two queen-sized beds," he said, "and we'll scarcely be in there except to sleep. Don't throw your money away on a second room, Linda."

She looked troubled. "Sharing a room with you wouldn't be smart, Matt."

"Are you worried about what you parents would think? About what Mrs. Wittmeyer would say if she found out?"

"No, that's not it."

He made his voice deliberately mocking. "Linda, I've passed the stage where the mere sight of a woman in my bedroom turns me into a slavering sex maniac. If you want to know whether I still find you desirable, the answer's definitely yes. I wanted you seven years ago, and I still want you now. A lot. But nothing will happen in that room tonight unless you want it to happen."

The look Linda gave him was very direct. "I know, and that's why I'm scared. It's me I'm afraid of, Matt, not you. It's always been me."

For once, Matt found himself at a loss for words. He'd been prepared for anything from Linda—except honesty. That he didn't know how to handle.

The lawyer, Barry Lendel, greeted them in the small conference room he'd arranged to have set aside for their use. He was clearly stunned by Linda's beauty, and Matt felt a little twist of proud amusement when Barry —a hard-core Manhattan sophisticate who considered Brooklyn Heights at the outer limits of the universe— almost fell over his feet escorting Linda to a chair.

"Mrs. Petrie, it's a pleasure to meet you," the lawyer said, polishing his horn-rimmed glasses. "A real pleasure. And may I say how delightful I found your sketches of the Rumbles, quaint little creatures that I'm sure will have great appeal in the soft-toy market. The patterns you've developed for their faces are most ingenious. The president of our company, Charles Bowen, was excited when he received the samples of your work in the mail. Even if Mr. Deighton hadn't expressed the opinion that your—"

"Do you have a preliminary draft of the contract for Mrs. Petrie to look at?" Matt asked quickly.

"Yes, certainly. I have it right here." Barry drew out duplicate copies of at least twenty legal-sized pages. "This is triple-spaced," he explained apologetically. "The final document won't appear quite so long."

Step by step, Matt went over the contract with Linda. To his relief, he saw that Charlie had outlined very fair terms, including an advance of ten thousand dollars, and a royalty of five percent on the wholesale price of each Rumble sold.

Linda read the contract very carefully. Matt soon discovered that her wits hadn't rusted despite living all her life in Carson. She asked a few questions, all of them pertinent, then listed eleven contract clauses that she felt needed amendments. Matt, a battered veteran of contract negotiations, agreed with every one of her points.

Barry Lendel naturally would have preferred a contract entirely in Playbrite's favor, but he was prepared to be reasonable, and over four hours of hard negotiations and many phone calls, they eventually reached an acceptable compromise on each of the disputed clauses.

When the final difference of opinion had been hammered out, Barry leaned back in his chair and mopped his brow. "Then everything is agreed, Mrs. Petrie? You'll sign a contract on these terms? You'll design clothes for each Rumble, and once you've approved the storyline, you'll illustrate any books we may publish about the Rumbles?"

Linda gave the lawyer a smile so full of pride and happiness that Matt felt his heart contract with an odd leap of shared excitement. "Yes," she said quietly. "I'll sign a contract on those terms."

Barry beamed and ordered a magnum of champagne. With the superefficient service the Westin prided itself on, the giant bottle arrived moments later. They finished the bottle while initialing a preliminary agreement and settling the details of when and where the final contracts would be signed.

Matt was fairly certain that Linda wasn't keeping track of how much champagne she'd consumed, but he didn't attempt to stop Barry filling her glass. Today of all days, she'd earned the right to get a little tipsy if she wanted to.

Displaying surprising tact, Barry Lendel refused Matt's halfhearted suggestion that he should join them for dinner. "There's a seven-thirty flight out of Stapleton Airport that I might make if I run," he said, gathering papers and pushing them into his briefcase. He held out his hand. "Good-bye, Mrs. Petrie. It's been a great pleasure meeting somebody so talented."

When he left the room, Linda stretched languorously and yawned. "I'm exhausted," she said. "Drained of every last scrap of energy. Do you think the hotel would mind if I fell asleep here in the chair?"

"Some food will revive you," Matt said, remembering a little too late that they'd eaten nothing all day. If he'd remembered earlier, he'd never have allowed Linda to swig so much champagne on an empty stomach. He pulled her to her feet. "What about that lobster you promised yourself? We're supposed to be getting ready for a celebratory dinner."

She slumped against his chest. "I'm too tired to eat," she protested, yawning again as if to prove her point.

Matt stroked her hair in an unthinking caress. "A shower will help," he said, his voice soft and inexplicably husky. "Wouldn't you like a shower before dinner?"

Linda peered up at him, her stance wobbly. "Whoops," she said, clutching the front of his shirt. She gave a little giggle. "My legs won't stay straight." She giggled again, a soft, ladylike sort of giggle. "Matt, I can't walk properly."

He put his arm around her waist and led her to the elevators. He suddenly felt disgusted with himself. Why in the world had he let Barry keep her champagne glass constantly filled? Despite the deceptive calm of Linda's outward appearance, he had known how overwrought and excited she was. He'd known she was swallowing the champagne without paying the slightest attention to her actions. He should have stopped her, not encouraged her to get drunk.

They stepped into the elevator, Linda tottering at his side. Matt was repelled by the niggling thought that maybe he'd kept her champagne glass filled because he'd known seducing her would be easier if she were a little bit drunk.

He hoped he hadn't sunk that low. Surely he couldn't be so hung up on the events of a long-gone summer that he would make love to a woman who needed to be drunk in order to respond to him? True, he wanted to shake Linda loose from a few of her small-town, old-fashioned inhibitions, but he wanted to seduce her and give her pleasure, not take advantage of her lousy head for alcohol.

"Shower time," he said, as soon as they were safely inside their room. He propped her up against the wall and opened the bathroom door.

Linda ignored him. She wobbled across the room and threw herself onto the nearer of the two beds. She crossed her legs neatly at the ankle, smoothed out her long, silky dress, and folded her hands on top of her stomach. "No shower," she said with great dignity. "I think I'll take a little nap instead."

Gently, Matt lifted her off the bed. "Honey, take my word for it. You'll feel better if you shower."

Linda's head flopped onto his shoulder. In a small voice, she asked him, "Matt, am I drunk?"

"Only a tiny bit." Still supporting her, he led her into the bathroom and turned on the shower, testing the water until it ran warm, but not too hot. He unwrapped a bar of soap and set it in the dish, then popped a disposable shower cap over her hair. How incredibly neat she still looked, even though she was tipsy. Matt found himself wondering what it would be like to stroke away Linda's smooth outer shell and discover the sensual woman who lay hidden somewhere deep inside the conventional covering. Surely the passionate girl he had known was still there, buried beneath the layers of repressed, puritanical woman?

Linda started to play with one of his shirt buttons, and he hastily reined in his wandering thoughts. "Can you manage to wash yourself?" he asked, lifting her head from where it had collapsed back against his chest.

"Yes."

She made no attempt to move, and he ran a washcloth under the cold tap, squeezed it awkwardly with one hand, and pressed it to her face. "Linda, either you get yourself undressed and under that shower, or I'll do it for you."

She blinked, but gave no other sign that she'd heard him. He sighed and tossed the washcloth into the sink. Carefully avoiding any contact with her skin, he reached around to find the zipper at the back of her dress. Slowly, he drew the zipper downward. When the dress was open to her waist, the sleeves began to fall off her shoulders.

Either the cold washcloth on her cheeks or the cold

air on her spine achieved the desired sobering effect. Linda slowly pulled herself out of his arms.

"I can manage by myself now," she said.

It was the steam that was making him feel so damned hot, Matt decided; it couldn't be anything else. He'd been with too many desirable women to get hot and bothered over a woman who probably still made love like a virgin. He cleared his throat. "I'll make a few phone calls while I'm waiting for you," he said.

He edged out of the bathroom and closed the door, listening for a moment until he heard the rustle of silk as she stepped out of her dress. He walked quickly to the other side of the room, his thoughts mocking him. Good grief, but he was a fool! He felt nothing for Linda except a simple, straightforward physical attraction.

So why hadn't he taken advantage of her obvious willingness to make love with him? Why did he feel this unfamiliar, aching tenderness at the thought of taking Linda into his bed?

Matt reached down and checked the air conditioning. He turned it up to full blast.

Chapter Seven

By THE TIME she stepped out of the shower and wrapped herself in one of the fluffy towels, the last of Linda's champagne-induced euphoria had fizzled away. Strangely enough, she didn't feel flat, or let down, or even hungover. Instead, she felt oddly tense, almost brittle, as if one wrong word or misplaced gesture might cause her body to shatter into a thousand pieces.

She took a hand towel and wiped the bathroom mirror. Her face stared back at her, pale and slightly fuzzy around the edges where stream blurred the reflection.

Fuzzy around the edges. That just about summed up her whole life, Linda thought. Here she was, twenty-five years old, widowed and the mother of two, yet she still seemed unable to take the initiative in anything unless her parents and the whole town of Carson turned out and cheered.

Even when she had married Jim, she had simply done what was expected of her. It wasn't until after the honeymoon that she realized how incredibly selfish her actions had been. The intimacy of marriage soon revealed what virtually any high school student could have told her: Jim Petrie was something more than a minister and a nice guy. He was a person in his own right, with needs and feelings Linda had totally ignored in deciding to marry him. He loved her. She had never loved him. After his death, when she looked back over their life together, she had felt overwhelmed by her inadequacy as a wife. Only the twins had saved her sanity. Thank God she had given Jim the twins! At least she had brought one measure of joy into a life she had otherwise made utterly miserable.

With an impatient gesture, Linda reached up and tore off her shower cap. She tugged at the pins holding her French twist in place, shaking out the heavy, shoulder-length waves. Twelve hours had gone by since she fixed her hair this morning, and not a strand or a curl had moved out of place. Even her hair was well behaved, Linda reflected with a flash of bitter self-mockery. Little Miss Perfect from curling head to pink-polished toes.

For a few moments this afternoon, she had thought she might finally be able to break out of the cage she had allowed the citizens of Carson to build around her. Like wind rushing through a tunnel, clearing out debris, she'd suddenly accepted the fact that other people's opinions didn't matter. Nobody else could decide what was right for her, because nobody else knew how she felt about Matt. Made courageous by the champagne, she'd finally admitted to herself how much she wanted to make love with him.

Of course, her grand seduction scene had failed miserably. Totally unused to alcohol, she'd practically fallen asleep on her feet, and Matt—darn his integrity—had refused to take advantage of her. And now she was stone-cold sober once again. A great way to be, if only her courage hadn't evaporated along with the champagne bubbles.

Linda seized her toothbrush and attacked her teeth with excessive vigor. She wished she were still a little bit drunk so she could slide into Matt's bed and pretend she didn't realize what she was doing. Except that Matt probably wouldn't cooperate in the deception. She had a suspicion she'd have to walk naked into his arms and say, "Here I am, take me," before he would make love to her.

Linda gave the mirror another swipe with the hand towel and glared at her reflection. Was it really that difficult to be honest about her own needs? Why didn't she tell Matt that she wanted him to make love to her? Wasn't that the way women were supposed to do things nowadays?

Her mirror image looked so appalled at this daring train of thought that Linda would have laughed if she hadn't felt so miserable. There was a neat sort of irony in her situation, she thought. If she became tipsy enough to lose her inhibitions, she couldn't remain awake. But without a haze of alcohol to give her false courage, she remained too uptight to make the necessary first move.

Linda combed her fingers nervously through her hair, wondering if she would ever work up the courage to walk out of the bathroom and say, "Take me to bed, Matt, I want you to make love to me. My body aches for you and for the memory of what we once shared."

Her reflection turned bright red, and Linda bit back a despairing gasp of laughter. Good grief, she was so inhibited, she couldn't even think the words, much less speak them!

A knock sounded at the door and she jumped, causing the towel to slip. She grabbed for it, trying to fix the knot as Matt's voice floated through the crack of the doorjamb. "Linda, are you still alive in there?"

I'm not going to think, she decided recklessly. *I'm only going to feel.* Drawing in a deep breath, she opened the door.

"I'm still alive. Sorry I took so long." Her smile, which was meant to appear bright and sophisticated, felt perilously like that of Bozo the Clown—painted and artificial.

"I thought the champagne might have done you in."

"Oh, no, I'm fine, thanks. No problems." Linda's mouth stretched into an even more Bozo-like smile. She shifted from one foot to the other, staring at her toes as if she'd never seen them before. She had no idea what to do next. Not thinking might be a great strategy for women with lots of experience, but it didn't work so well for somebody whose knowledge of seduction techniques could fit easily into a thimble.

She finally gathered the nerve to glance up. Matt was looking at her in a way that made the blood turn to fire in her veins.

"Linda?" he murmured, his voice hoarse as he said her name.

"I've missed you," she replied, without giving herself time to have doubts. "So very much."

"I missed you, too. More than I knew until I came home to Carson. We shared something special, didn't we?"

"We were in love," she said simply.

"Yes, we were, until the good citizens of Carson spoiled it." He reached out and ran the tip of his fingers along the edge of the towel, his eyes dark with memories. Linda's heart beat more rapidly as she felt a half-familiar, half-forgotten ribbon of heat unfurl in the wake of his touch. When his fingers reached the knot holding the towel in place, he hesitated.

"Linda?" he said again.

Scarcely daring to breathe, she moved forward until their bodies touched, trapping his hand against her breast. His fingers were cool, but heat radiated out from his touch, and desire arrowed straight to the core of her being.

"Matt," she whispered. "Oh, yes, Matt, please."

He made a harsh sound deep in his throat, but to her disappointment he didn't attempt to remove the towel. His free hand brushed very lightly over her hair and then he drew away.

"Linda, God knows I want you, but I'm not sure this is the right time for us. You drank five glasses of champagne this afternoon. You haven't eaten all day—"

"I'm not drunk, Matt. I know what I'm doing."

"Do you? Maybe this is more dangerous for us emotionally now than it was seven years ago. You've been married, and I've been around the block a couple of times. We have enough experience to hurt each other, Linda. Hurt each other badly."

"And we didn't hurt each other seven years ago? Funny, I always thought that we did."

He didn't answer and she smiled, although she could feel tears tightening her throat. "You took my virginity, Matt; now I'm asking you to give me something back. Make love to me. Make me feel like a woman again."

Heat flared darkly along his cheekbones as he looked down at her. He cradled her hips in his hands and pulled her roughly against his body. "That's what you do to me, Linda," he said huskily. "You're a beautiful and desirable woman, and I have all the usual male appetites. If you keep asking, I'm going to give you what you're asking for. Last chance, Linda. Are you sure you really want this to happen? When we wake up tomorrow morning, I don't want you to regret this."

She astonished herself by laughing. "Matt, you're stealing my lines. Isn't it the woman who's supposed to protest all the way to the bed?" She pressed her finger against his lips. She felt teasing, provocative, *womanly*. "I'll still respect you in the morning, Matt, I promise."

He didn't respond to her smile. His gaze remained somber as he looked at her, although she could feel the hardness of his body stir against her, and his face was taut with wanting. "You have it all wrong, Linda. The real question isn't whether you'll respect *me*. It's whether you'll respect yourself."

She didn't want to think about what he was saying. She didn't want to make difficult moral decisions. She wanted him to take her into his arms and tell her that he loved her. She wanted him to seduce her with burning words and passionate kisses. Oh, God, how she wished at this moment that he would lie! That he would tell her their lovemaking had lived all these years in his memory, surpassing his experience with every other woman.

But why did she need him to lie? Linda asked herself. Why did she always want somebody else to take responsibility for her actions? It was her own feelings that mattered, and she knew exactly how she felt about Matt, even if she couldn't bring herself to admit the betraying words into her mind. Given the way she felt, anybody else's approval seemed of zero importance in the greater scheme of things. In a gesture totally at odds with her usual behavior, she stood on tiptoe, silencing Matt's questions with a kiss.

For a split second, he resisted, then his mouth slanted across hers, moving with hot, seeking urgency as he took control of their embrace. His tongue caressed her mouth with sinful skill, and a sunburst of pleasurable sensations radiated through her body.

"You like that?" he murmured, catching her lip lightly between his teeth.

"Yes." It was all she could say. For pride's sake, she would have liked to conceal the devastating effect of his kisses, but hunger for his lovemaking had long since outweighed any notions of pride.

He smiled, satisfied with her reaction, unknotting the towel with casual expertise and letting it fall in a pool at her feet. His hand brushed over her naked breasts, circling her nipples. Her whole body tingled when he finally cupped the weight of her breast in his palm.

"You grew," he said, whispering the words hoarsely against her mouth.

"The babies . . . the twins . . ."

His fingers resumed their stroking. "They made you more beautiful than before." He bent his head and drew his lips over her nipples, moistening them with his tongue until they stood out firm and throbbing against the heavy fullness of her breasts.

Linda closed her eyes, surrendering to the magic of Matt's touch. This was what she had dreamed of for seven long years. She slid her hands over his back, reveling in the feel of his shirt stretched tautly over muscles hardened by physical labor. He kissed her again, and she drank the taste of him into her mouth. At last she was in his arms once more, and nothing had felt this right since that distant summer when he'd covered her body with his own and held her under the stars.

She was mindless with pleasure by the time he carried her to the bed. She watched through half-closed eyes as he took off his clothes, reacquainting herself with the strong lines of his body. He looked older, stronger . . . and infinitely more desirable.

When he joined her on the bed, her hips arched to his touch in a reflex as old as time and as new as this night's passion. Their naked bodies touched from shoulder to thigh, and Linda felt him tremble. She experienced a tiny surge of feminine triumph that she still retained the power to make this man want her with such powerful urgency.

He pressed her head back against the pillows, capturing her mouth as his hands roamed enticingly over her narrow waist and flat stomach. When his fingers at last slipped between her thighs, Linda didn't even try to choke back her little moan of delight.

Even in the darkness, she could feel his smile. He nuzzled her ear. "I think I just discovered something else you like me to do."

She buried her face in his neck. "I don't know," she mumbled, scarcely able to speak. "Try it again, and we'll see."

"A scientific experiment, hmm?" His fingers resumed their teasing, and she gasped with pleasure. Matt laughed softly. "I guess we proved you like it. Shall we stop the experiment?"

"No." It was all she could say, but her hand moved across the flat plane of his stomach and clasped the hardness of his erection. She stroked him as he was stroking her.

"How about you, Matt?" she asked, shocked by her own daring. "Want to join the experiment? How does it feel when I touch you like this?"

Sweat beaded his forehead, and he groaned his answer. "Linda, sweetheart, what you're doing is wonderful, but keep it up and this isn't going to last much longer."

After years of unfulfilled sexual need, her body ached for ultimate release, but Linda was so grateful for the passion Matt had aroused in her that she almost didn't care whether or not he brought her to climax. Sexual relations during her marriage had been so disastrous that she'd begun to wonder if she was clinically frigid. The knowledge that she could be so thoroughly aroused was balm to her soul even if her body was destined to remain frustrated. "If you're ready, Matt, we don't have to wait for me," she said softly.

He took her mouth in a kiss that was almost savage. "Oh, no, you don't, honey. I'm not the least bit interested in sharing my bed with a martyr. I want tonight to be as good for you as it is for me."

He captured her hands above her head and moved against her, warm and hard and compelling. She looked up, delighting in seeing him cradled over her, his eyes dark and glowing with the joy her body was giving him. A fine mist dewed her skin, and her breath quickened. The knowledge of how she was affecting Matt added the final spur of urgency to her own desire. She writhed in his grasp, trying to pull him into her, but he resisted, caressing her again with his hand until she quivered uncontrollably, poised on the very edge of climax.

"Now you're ready, sweetheart." His penetration was swift and deep, carrying them both to the brink of fulfillment. Still he held himself back, moving slowly until she arched against him, crying out his name and begging feverishly for release. At last he contained himself no longer, and the tempo of his thrusts increased.

Linda buried her face in his neck, clinging to him as the incredible spasms rocked through her. The bed, the hotel room, the world, all faded into blackness as Matt took her with him into ecstasy.

Linda never did get her lobster for dinner. At some stage during the evening—her sense of timing became a bit hazy after the second time they made love—Matt called room service and ordered hamburgers, french fries, and iced tea for two. Their meal was wheeled in on a linen-draped trolley, decorated with starched damask napkins, and the ketchup and mustard served in engraved silver sauce boats.

Matt dismissed the white-gloved waiter with a generous tip and pulled the serving cart alongside one of the beds.

"I'm starving," Linda announced as they curled up

side by side on the bed. She leaned back against the pillows and munched the french fry Matt dangled in front of her.

"These fries are almost as good as McDonald's," he remarked, catching a drip of ketchup expertly in his napkin.

"Mmm . . ." Linda dragged herself up from the pillows and leaned over to peer at the bill. "Good grief, Matt!" she exclaimed, nearly choking on her poppy-seed bun. "This ought to be the best meal we've ever eaten! Did you see how much they charged us?"

Matt took the bill and tossed it in the direction of his discarded clothes. "My treat," he said. "Enjoy your dinner and stop worrying about prices, Linda."

She grimaced. "Force of habit, I guess. But let me pay for this, since I'm the one who just made a big sale—"

Matt seemed absorbed in slathering mustard on his burger. "Look, maybe it's time to get something straight. It's Mrs. Wittmeyer, not me, who told everybody I'm out of work and down to my last penny. Like a hell of a lot of other things Mrs. Wittmeyer passes out as gospel, this snippet of news just isn't true. I'm not down to my last penny, Linda, I'm not even down to my last few hundred dollars. I can easily afford to buy us dinner."

She smiled. "Even if the french fries cost a dollar a piece?"

"Even then. Even if they cost two dollars a piece." Matt reclined against the pillows, and squinted at her through lazily drooping eyelids. "Let's stop discussing money. Draw me a picture of two Rumbles who've just made glorious love."

"Rumbles don't make love," she said, trying to sound reproving. "Rumbles are family-oriented creatures."

"Then how do they get baby Rumbles?"

"The stork delivers them, of course. Rumbles are very sedate."

He grinned. "Not when they make love, they aren't. I have firsthand experience. When Rumbles make love, they go hog-wild."

She blushed. "Who invented them, Matthew Deighton? I did, that's who. And I assure you, the Rumbles don't make love."

He rolled over onto his side and blew gently across her breasts. "Now they do," he said, waiting until her nipples came erect, and then glancing up at her with laughing eyes. "For seven years, they forgot how, but they just rediscovered the magic. Draw me my very own pair of Rumbles, Linda. Please?"

"Oh, all right then!" She got off the bed and hunted around to find a piece of hotel stationery and a suitable pencil, as much to put some distance between herself and Matt as for any other reason. Once she started drawing, however, the power of her imagination took over. She worked hard for ten minutes, then tossed the resulting sketch onto Matt's stomach. "Well, what do you think?"

There was a long pause. "I think you're unbelievably talented," he said finally. "I also thank you for the compliment."

She snatched the paper back and stared at it accusingly. "Compliment?" she demanded. "Didn't you notice how revoltingly self-satisfied Mr. Rumble looks? The silly creature obviously thinks he's God's gift to womankind."

"I noticed," Matt replied softly. "But I also noticed the dazzled expression on Ms. Rumble's face. Mr. Rumble may be an arrogant macho bastard, but I think he's been showing his lady friend a pretty good time. Am I wrong?"

Linda scowled, embarrassed at how much she had

unwittingly revealed. "She's just being polite. Female Rumbles are always polite. Even in the presence of arrogant macho bastards."

"Are they?" Matt pulled apart the lapels of Linda's robe and began to stroke an exotic trail toward her waist. "You know what? I think Ms. Rumble's politeness is all a façade. Underneath that demure exterior of hers, I think there's an incredibly passionate and independent woman waiting to break free."

Linda laid her hands on his chest and smiled ruefully. "If there is, it'll do her no good. You should know by now that the only thing Carson dislikes more than a passionate woman is an independent one. Ms. Rumble's going to have to get her act together again before she goes home."

"Maybe," he said, his expression hard to read. "But tonight there's just you and me, Linda. Don't think about tomorrow and what the people in Carson might say." He bent his head toward her mouth. "Think about this, honey. Tonight this is all there is."

She reached up, meeting his kiss as eagerly as he gave it. His hands moved down her body, shaping her breasts, her waist, her thighs. Her body blazed into exultant life, and he brought her hips under his, joining their bodies in the ultimate embrace. Her hands grasped his shoulders, then slid up into his hair, pulling his mouth hard against her lips. For a timeless moment, they were held suspended in the still center of a raging storm; then the passion exploded and the storm surged over then, carrying them drifting and exhausted to the haven on the other side.

The morning-after syndrome didn't hit Linda until she arrived back in Carson and found Mrs. Wittmeyer lying in wait, all ready to watch the Return of the Prodigal.

Matt escorted Linda to the front door of her parents'

home. Nora answered the first ring of the doorbell, giving Matt a curt nod and her daughter a flustered kiss. She burst immediately into nervous speech. "Greta Wittmeyer's here, waiting for you, Lindy Beth. Hello, Matt, how are you? Lindy Beth, I'm sorry, but the twins have just this minute gone out with your father to buy ice cream. When you were late back, they started to get anxious—"

"The plane was a half hour late," Matt explained. "I'm sorry, Nora. The public phones were all in use, and we decided it wasn't worth delaying even longer to give you a call."

"I'm sure you did what you thought was best, Matt. Come on in, why don't you? Did I tell you Greta Wittmeyer's here? Come into the living room. Did everything go smoothly?"

Linda smiled. "Better than smooth."

"You . . . you sold your drawings?"

"Oh, Mom, I have a contract with Playbrite! They're going to start manufacturing the first batch of Rumbles as soon as their Christmas production runs are finished. And I'm supposed to design clothes and illustrate storybooks and everything!"

"Oh, dear, oh, dear! Oh, I mean, that's wonderful, Lindy Beth. Congratulations." Nora couldn't have sounded more miserable if her daughter had announced the imminent end of civilization. She forced a pathetic attempt at a smile. "You'd better come into the living room while we wait for your father, Lindy Beth. You, too, Matt. Unless you need to get home?"

"I guess I can spare a few minutes to greet an old friend like Mrs. Wittmeyer."

Linda cast him a grateful look as they followed her mother into the living room. Mrs. Wittmeyer was ensconced on her favorite sofa, nose twitching and antennae quivering, ready to pick up any hint of scandal.

"Well, *hello*, Lindy Beth." Mrs. Wittmeyer gave an imperious nod of welcome that would have done credit to the queen of England. "We all wondered when you and Matt would be back from Denver. I must say you both look very pleased with yourselves."

Matt lounged against the doorway. "We are," he said coolly. "Didn't you hear what we were saying in the hallway, Mrs. Wittmeyer? Linda has sold her drawings to a major New York toy manufacturer."

"Well, fancy that. How nice for you, dear. Those people from New York do the strangest things, don't they?" Mrs. Wittmeyer obviously had no interest in pursuing a boring subject like Lindy Beth's success as an artist. "You left on the early-morning flight yesterday, and it took you all day and all night to hammer out the contract details, did it?"

"No, not at all," Matt replied, smiling with false innocence. "We finished the contract negotiations late yesterday afternoon. Linda and I decided to stay on in Denver and celebrate her success with a special dinner."

"Would you like a cup of coffee?" Nora interjected. "And how about you, Greta? Didn't you mention something about needing to get home to let in the carpet cleaners?"

Mrs. Wittmeyer flashed her teeth in what passed for a smile. "I'm sure I can spare a few minutes to chat with dear little Lindy Beth after she's taken such an exciting trip. You look positively glowing, my dear. Not at all the same sad widow we knew only a couple of weeks ago. The air in Denver must work miracles. Or maybe it's the company you've been keeping? My, I never saw such a bloom on your cheeks even when you came

home from your honeymoon with poor dear Jim Petrie."
She sighed. "Such a hero, and gone forever now."

Disgust bubbled up inside Linda, gushing out like an
underground spring suddenly set free. "Exactly what are
you implying, Mrs. Wittmeyer?"

"Have a cookie," Nora interjected desperately.
"Would anybody like one of my icebox cookies?
They're Ron's favorites. He says they're delicious."

"No thank you, Nora, dear. Too much sugar is bad
for you. You should tell Ron to eat more fruit and not so
many baked goods. Why, Lindy Beth, whatever do you
mean, *what am I implying?* I wasn't implying anything.
Except that your night in Denver seems to have done
you a world of good."

Linda's anger was still in full spate. Her normal
meekness seemed to have disappeared into a black hole,
never to return. She stared at Mrs. Wittmeyer defiantly.
"Actually, you're quite right," she said. "Matt and I *did*
have a wonderful time in Denver, and it *has* done me a
world of good. We had an outstanding time together."

"And where did you have dinner, dear? I don't think
you said?"

"In bed." Linda smiled—a Mrs. Wittmeyer-like
smile, dazzling in its insincerity. "We ate dinner in bed
and then spent the entire night making mad, passionate
love to each other. Do you know, Matt showed me ways
to make love that I'd never even dreamed of. In fact, we
practically had an orgy going on in our room."

"Lindy Beth—!"

Linda ignored the strangled shriek from her mother.
She felt as if the weight of years was tumbling from her
back. "Is that what you wanted to hear?" she demanded
of Mrs. Wittmeyer. "Do you want more details of exactly how Matt and I made love, or have I given you
enough ammunition to see you through the next two or

three coffee parties? Believe me, if you're not satisfied, there's lots more I could say!"

Nora Owen stared at her daughter as if she were seeing her for the first time. The plate of icebox cookies trembled in her grasp. Meanwhile, Mrs. Wittmeyer rose to her feet, purse clutched to her stomach, the picture of outraged womanhood.

"Lindy Beth, I'm surprised at you. I don't find your childish attempts at humor in very good taste. Apart from anything else, I thought you had more sense than to indulge in that sort of nasty loose talk. I realize you're joking, of course, but no woman's reputation is ever completely safe, and somebody without my experience of the world might believe the nonsense you're talking. Now, if you'll see me to the door, Nora, I would like a word with you in private. *Somebody* is exerting a very undesirable influence over Lindy Beth."

"Yes, of course, Greta. I'll walk you to the gate." Nora cast an anguished look in her daughter's direction and scurried from the room. "Lindy Beth, don't you go away," she pleaded. "I'll be right back."

Matt scarcely waited until the two older woman were out of the room before breaking into laughter. "Well done, honey! You were terrific. I never thought I'd live to see Mrs. Wittmeyer at a loss for words!"

Linda pressed her hands to her burning cheeks. "Matt, I can't believe what I just did!"

"You told Mrs. Wittmeyer to mind her own business, that's all. Nothing very dreadful in that."

"But to be so rude to somebody in my mother's house!"

Matt took her hands and squeezed them gently. "It was Mrs. Wittmeyer who was rude, Linda. You just called her on her rudeness, and she's not accustomed to that." He dropped a swift kiss on the end of her nose.

"Honey, I have to make a couple of urgent phone calls to New York. Take care of yourself. I'll stop by and see you tomorrow."

A little chill squeezed tight around Linda's heart, but she managed to produce a smile. She had known all along that their night of lovemaking wouldn't mean anything earth-shattering to Matt, so she'd had plenty of time to prepare herself for the inevitable casualness of his parting. "I'll understand if you're too busy to come over," she said. "Anyway, I'll be pretty busy myself catching up on things."

He caught her face between his hands and kissed her in a way that was anything but casual. "I'll stop by tomorrow," he said. "I won't be too busy. Not for you." He brushed his thumbs gently across her cheeks. "Thank you for last night," he said softly. "You were beautiful, Linda. You made me feel very special."

He rumpled her hair and strode down the path to his car, whistling. Linda was still standing at the door when her mother came into the kitchen.

"What is it?" Nora asked sharply. "What's happened? Why are you crying?"

Linda reached for a tissue. "Just tired, I guess."

"Tired? Didn't you sleep last night? Why didn't you sleep last night?"

Linda didn't answer, and for once her mother was smart enough not to ask any more questions.

Chapter Eight

LINDA WAS SITTING in a garden lounge chair, reading Kate a story and watching Drew dig holes at the corner of the patio, when Matt came to call the next morning. He wore scuffed sneakers, threadbare cutoffs, and a paint-spattered T-shirt. A faded logo on his shirt advertised *Legend of the Witch*, a musical that had taken Broadway by storm two seasons earlier. Despite the tattered clothes, Linda thought she had never seen a man who looked more confident or more sexually appealing.

Kate wasn't pleased to have her favorite story interrupted while her mother daydreamed. She tossed a cursory "Hi!" in Matt's direction, then jiggled up and down on Linda's lap. "Read more, Mommy," she instructed, pointing to the book.

"I'd like to hear the story, too," Matt said, pulling up a chair. "May I listen while your mom reads to you, Kate?"

Kate surveyed him for several seconds before giving grudging permission. "You can listen," she said. "But don't talk."

Linda finished the Dr. Seuss story of Sam who discovers that he loves green eggs and ham when he finally agrees to taste them. As soon as the last word of the story had been read, Kate leaned over and rifled back to the beginning of the book. "Read it again, Mommy!" she demanded.

"Kate, we've read it three times today already," Linda protested, sighing with relief when Drew provided a diversion by walking up to Matt and offering him something he'd dug out of the ground. Even Dr. Seuss became hard to take the fourth time around.

"For you," Drew said, holding out his cupped, filthy hands.

"Thank you very much." Matt accepted the two dead beetles with every appearance of equanimity. "This is an interesting present," he commented. "Did you find them in the garden?"

"Yes." Drew squirmed up onto Matt's lap. Shy with most adults, he seemed to have accepted Matt as a comfortable fixture on his landscape. "Why don't they fly away?" he asked.

"Their wings are hidden under those shiny black cases. They have to open up the cases before they can fly."

"Then why don't they do it?" Drew persisted. "Don't they want to fly?"

"They can't fly anymore," Matt explained matter-of-factly. "These beetles are dead, Drew."

Drew scowled. He grabbed the beetles from Matt's hand and flung them angrily toward the hedge. "Dead is nasty," he said. "My daddy is dead. He is goned away for ever."

"He is in heaven," Kate corrected.

"But he can't come back," Drew said, for once not allowing his sister the final word. "He is goned away."

Linda's stomach knotted with pain. It always disturbed her when her twins parroted back comments they had absorbed from the adults around them without really understanding what they were saying. Jim had been such a wonderful father, she bitterly regretted that the twins had no personal memories to cherish him by.

Matt flashed her a look that warmed her with its sympathy. He held Drew a little bit closer. "Your dad was a very brave and special person. Everybody in Carson misses him a lot. He loved you and Kate very much, you know that, don't you? He didn't want to leave you."

Kate, ever practical, didn't seem able to sustain interest in a father she didn't remember, but her mother was a different matter altogether. She squirmed around to look anxiously at Linda. "You won't die, will you, Mommy?"

"No," Linda said quickly, deciding this was an occasion when fudging the truth was more desirable than total honesty. "No, I'm going to be here for you and Drew as long as you need me, I promise."

"You went away," Drew pointed out accusingly. "You went away to Denv'r."

"But I came back, didn't I? Denver isn't very far away, you know. One day, when you're a bit bigger, I'll take you there."

Drew's worried expression lightened, and he jumped off Matt's lap. "Do they have ice cream in Denv'r?"

"Lots and lots of ice cream. All different kinds. More than at Scoop-a-Doop."

"Choklec ice cream?"

"Chocolate *and* fudge ripple. And pink bubble-gum flavor."

Drew appeared more than satisfied with this response. "Are you coming to Denv'r, Katie?"

"No." Kate had no intention of falling in with one of her brother's suggestions, and she hastened to reassert her superiority. "We're staying here. We are firsty. We want Kool-Aid."

"I'm not firsty," Drew protested.

"We're *both* firsty," Kate said firmly. "Come on, Drew. We want Kool-Aid from Granny."

Drew sighed, then obediently trotted off behind his sister in search of a drink. "I hope I said the right thing," Matt commented as soon as the twins were out of earshot.

"Yes, thank you, what you said was fine. A child psychologist told us we could say almost anything that felt right, as long as we encouraged the children to speak about their father. As a matter of fact, they rarely mention him. I'm glad to know they at least think about him occasionally."

"I expect they'll ask more questions when they're older. They're still hardly more than babies." Matt leaned back in his chair, stretching his long, tanned legs out in front of him. "Jennifer called last night," he said. "She asked me to tell you hi."

"Her morning newscast is getting terrific reviews," Linda said, grateful for the change of subject.

"Yes, she's pleased about that, although it doesn't seem to be the subject uppermost in her mind right now."

"What's going on with her?"

"Doug Hotchkiss," Matt replied with a grin. "Jennifer spent ten minutes talking about her show and the best part of an hour telling me how wonderful Doug Hotchkiss is. That was in between insisting at two-minute intervals that she wasn't going to talk about him anymore."

Linda smiled. "They were practically melting into one another's arms at the airport last week. Do you think they're really serious about each other?"

"Jennifer actually mumbled something about September being a good month for a wedding. She backtracked like crazy when she realized what she'd said, but it sounds pretty serious to me."

"That's great. I'm so pleased for them. The odd thing is, I think they're really suited to each other."

"So do I, and my parents are thrilled. My mother's holed up in her studio, painting them a personalized dinner service!"

Linda laughed. "How much do you bet she'll insist on a church wedding with bridesmaids and the whole bit? I think every mother turns traditionalist when it's time for her children to get married."

"I wouldn't bet against you. Mom tries hard to shock Carson, but she's really a conservative at heart."

"You'd better watch out, Matt! Any day now she'll start bugging you to find a 'nice girl' and settle down."

He grinned, unconcerned. "Oh, she's been doing that for years. She keeps telling me I'll never find the right woman if I don't improve the company I keep. I've a hunch that deep down my mother views New York City with almost as much suspicion as yours."

Linda rolled her eyes. "For heaven's sake, don't ever say that to your mom's face! She'll never forgive you. She cherishes her reputation as a rebel."

He laughed, and then his expression sobered. "I'm going away for a few days, Linda. Doug Hotchkiss has offered to loan me his house in Grand Junction, since he'll be in Denver with my sister. I have a project I'm working on that needs some space."

"I've heard Doug's house is gorgeous. Mrs. Wittmeyer knows the builder's nephew, and she reported that there's a pool in the backyard with an overhanging grotto and a cascading waterfall. We were all terribly impressed when we realized just how successful Doug the Nerd had become."

"Mmm, he said something about a pool, and a Jacuzzi in the master bedroom. But its major attraction as far as I'm concerned is the space. I still haven't learned how to paint unless I have lots of room."

This was the only time Matt had mentioned his painting since his return home. Linda responded eagerly. "You're starting work on another painting?"

"Yes. On a series, as a matter of fact."

"Matt, don't keep me in suspense! Do you have a commission?"

"Yeah, I guess I do."

Her smile felt as if it stretched from ear to ear. "Gosh, has this ever been a fantastic week! First me, now you. We're both going to be famous commercial artists before the year's out! Matt, I'm so happy for you! Congratulations."

He glanced at her rather oddly. "You really care, don't you? But you never asked about my painting, Linda. Why not?"

"I didn't want to probe something that might be painful for you," she admitted. "You seemed so uncomfortable whenever I mentioned your work that I was afraid to pry."

His gaze continued to hold hers, but he didn't speak, and tension arced suddenly between them. The heavy silence became filled with the chirp of cicadas and the steady rumble of cars on the distant highway. "Come away with me, Linda," he said abruptly. "Spend the next few days with me in Grand Junction. We could make it good for both of us."

Her breath caught in reckless anticipation, and she almost said yes. Heaven knew, she was tempted to accept, to allow herself to experience the joy of Matt's lovemaking one more time before the inevitable end. For once, it wasn't concern over what her parents or the townsfolk might say that held her back. It was fear of

Matt's power to hurt her. His lifestyle had no room in it for a wife and two ready-made children, whereas her lifestyle had no room in it for casual affairs. Matt would be leaving Carson in a few days, and if she wanted to emerge from their encounter relatively unscathed, she would be wise to preserve what tiny shreds of common sense she still retained.

But you could have an affair with him, some unregenerate part of her whispered. *You could see him in New York. This time, you wouldn't have to wait another seven years for him to come back to Carson. With all the work that needs to be done on the Rumbles, you could invent an excuse-a-month for trips to the East Coast.*

The idea was so tempting that it frightened her. "No," she said quickly. "Thanks for the invitation, Matt, but I really can't come. You heard what Drew said about my trip to Denver. I'm a single parent, and I have special responsibilities to the twins. I need to stay home with them."

"That's an excuse, Linda, not a reason. If you never go away, even for a couple of nights, the twins won't have the chance to learn that you always come back."

"The twins are only a part of it," Linda said, surprising herself by the relative ease with which she confessed the truth. She looked up, not trying to mask her inner turmoil. "It wouldn't be smart for me to go away with you, Matt. I know I'm old-fashioned, but I can't cope with a casual affair. I'm not sure I even want to."

He leaned over and plucked a strand of grass from the edge of the patio. "We're not having a casual affair. We've known each other too long and been too important to each other for that."

He seemed on the verge of saying something more, and she held her breath, hoping against hope that he might make some promise of a longer-term commitment. Of course he didn't. He chewed absently on the blade of grass, apparently absorbed in watching the progress of a high-flying cloud.

Linda sighed, chiding herself for adolescent fantasies. In the real world, men like Matt didn't suddenly abandon years of freewheeling living for the heavy-duty commitment of a wife and family. Once Matt left Carson, he probably wouldn't even be interested in pursuing a no-strings affair with her. Unless she'd taken total leave of her senses, she wouldn't deliberately put herself in a situation that could only cause pain.

Linda knew she was doing the right thing, but her throat ached with unshed tears when she gave him her answer. "Matt, I'm sorry, I can't come with you."

The strand of grass snapped, and he tossed it away. "We shared something special the other night," he commented quietly.

"Yes, we did." She drew in a deep breath. "Don't you see, Matt? I have to protect myself. Seven years ago, we let our passions control us, and we hurt each other. We're older now—don't you think we both ought to be a little wiser? If I come away with you . . . if we make love again . . . I know I'll get hurt." Her voice died away to a whisper. "I couldn't survive loving you again, Matt."

His mouth tightened. "What are you holding out for, Lindy Beth? A guarantee of a pain-free future? Somebody should have told you, there ain't no such thing."

She winced at the sarcastic way he inflected her nickname. She should have know better than to try to explain the truth of what she was feeling, she thought sadly. Hadn't she discovered as a child that nobody ever wanted to hear the truth about how she felt?

"You misunderstood, Matt," she said woodenly. "I'm

trying to behave sensibly. I'm not holding out for any-thing."

"Not even a wedding ring?" he asked, his voice still hard. "Funny. Judging from the past, I'd have thought a nice respectable gold band could tempt you into almost anything, Lindy Beth."

She got up from the garden chair and stood very straight, meeting him eye to eye. "A wedding ring from you would be the last thing to tempt me," she said quietly. "Marriage without love on both sides is unen-durable, I've already learned that lesson. Good-bye, Matt. Enjoy your stay in Grand Junction."

She turned and walked quickly toward the back door, avoiding flower tubs and garden furniture more by in-stinct than by conscious thought. Matt caught up with her almost immediately, and grasped her arm to stop her from entering the kitchen. "Linda, I'm sorry. My re-marks were way out of line. I wanted your company this weekend and was disappointed when you refused, so I threw a tantrum. Since I'm too old and ornery to send to my room, will you forgive me?"

"Forgiven," she said, hoping her smile didn't appear as tremulous as it felt. "Although I still think somebody should send you to your room to cool off."

Two small faces pressed themselves against the screen door. "Why are you pulling my mommy's arm?" Kate piped up as she came into the yard.

Matt muttered a short expletive under his breath, but he relaxed his grip on Linda's arm, sliding his hand downward to clasp lightly around her fingers. "I wasn't hurting your mom," he said. "I was talking to her. We're friends, so we like to touch each other some-times."

Drew hadn't left the kitchen, and he spoke from his perch behind the screen. "Why?"

"Because it feels good. Like when your mom gives you hugs."

Drew absorbed this answer in silence. "You want some Kool-Aid?" he asked finally. "It's red."

Matt's eyes twinkled. "I can see that from your mustache. Thanks for the offer, Drew, but I have to get home. I'm going on a trip, and I need to pack my suitcase."

"You're not going, are you, Mommy?" Kate asked quickly. "You're not taking her away, are you, Matt?"

"No," he said after a little pause. "Your mommy isn't coming with me, although I wish she would."

Drew came out of the kitchen and stared uncertainly at his sister. As if sensing something unusual in the atmosphere, he and Kate edged closer to Linda, clinging to her shorts and then reaching up in search of her hands.

Matt eyed their worried faces ruefully. "Outmaneuvered by the preschooler brigade," he murmured. Before Linda could protest, he leaned over the twins' heads and kissed her, his mouth hungry as he sought her lips. Fortunately for her good intentions, he didn't prolong the embrace. Hands resting on her shoulders, he lifted his head and spoke softly. "I'll be alone in Doug Hotchkiss's house until next Monday," he said. "If you should happen to change your mind about things, please join me. Don't let the twins hold you hostage."

Everything in her responded to the husky appeal in his voice. She longed to cast caution to the winds and accept his invitation. Perhaps, if the twins hadn't been clinging so tightly to her, she would have said yes. As it was, she somehow found the willpower to resist.

"Matt, it wouldn't work," she murmured. "Not for either of us."

"Caution doesn't always pay off, Linda. Sometimes

you have to turn a blind corner before you can find out what's ahead of you on the road."

"Maybe," she agreed sadly. "But if you're smart, you don't drive off the edge of a cliff you already know is there."

"I don't believe we're close to any cliffs; it feels too good when we're together." Not waiting for her reply, he bent down and gave each of the twins a quick hug. "Bye, kids. Keep cool, and I'll see you next week." Straightening, he touched Linda's cheek in a swift caress. "Don't run off with any handsome strangers while I'm gone."

"Ugly ones are okay?"

"No!" He appeared faintly surprised by the vehemence of his own answer. He hesitated for an instant, obviously on the brink of saying something significant, but at that moment, from inside the house, Nora called the twins. He frowned, pressed his finger against Linda's lips, then turned and strode quickly down the path toward the street.

For the rest of the day, Linda did her best to block out all thoughts of Matt. The most effective method of doing this was by working nonstop. To her relief, her parents attended their annual bowling league awards dinner, so she was able to avoid all but the most superficial conversation with them. However well they meant, right at this moment she wasn't up to hearing any more snide comments about how irresponsible Matt was, and what a good thing it would be for Carson when he returned to New York City.

Sleep proved elusive, and eventually she abandoned any hope of dozing off. She wandered over to her drafting table, and was soon engrossed in a series of preliminary designs for the Rumbles' clothes. In the stillness of the summer night, the creatures seemed more alive, more real, than they had ever been before, and gradually the idea for a story began to take shape in her mind.

The storyline unfolded in picture form, and she drew feverishly until dawn. By sunrise, she had created a small, make-believe town hidden away among the trees and grasses of New York's Central Park, and had invented an entire history of how the Rumbles had come to live there. She had no idea if Playbrite would accept either the illustrations or her story idea. The lawyer had made it clear that Playbrite planned to contract with a professional writer to invent a suitable background for the Rumbles. Nevertheless, when she examined her drawings in the cool light of morning, she knew that these illustrations displayed a creative urgency her work had rarely achieved in the past.

Bleary-eyed, still half caught up in the mythical world she had invented, Linda left her room only when it was time to help the twins prepare for breakfast. After they'd eaten, she felt too restless to play with them in the backyard, and she bundled them into the car and took off for a local amusement park. Once there, she spent a miserable day trying not to think about Matt, and the twins spent a marvelous day overdosing on cotton candy and making themselves dizzy on the merry-go-round.

Linda was in the bathroom, watching the twins splash in a sea of bubbles, when her mother came home from an afternoon of bridge with the ladies of Carson.

"I hear Matt Deighton has taken himself off to Grand Junction," Nora remarked, kneeling alongside her daughter and searching for a washcloth amid the foam.

Linda managed to suppress a sigh. She removed a layer of dirt and sticky pink sugar from Drew's neck. "Yes, he's staying in Doug Hotchkiss's house for a couple of days. How in the world do you think this son of mine got cotton candy inside his ears?"

"I don't know. I never allowed you to eat it. You'll ruin their teeth with all that sweet stuff."

"Yes, Mother."

"You look tired. Aren't you getting enough sleep?"

"I was working late last night."

"On those creatures of yours?"

"On the Rumbles, yes." Linda lifted Kate out of the tub and wrapped her in a towel. "Mom, could you please dry Drew?"

Nora took another towel and held out her arms to her grandson. She didn't hug him, or kiss him, but love shone in every line of her angular body. "So when's Matt coming back to Carson?" she asked, rubbing Drew's toes.

"I don't know. Monday or Tuesday, I guess."

"Nothing'll ever come of it, you know, Lindy Beth. It's no good you mooning after him. He's never going to marry you. He's not the type."

Linda reached behind her for Kate's nightshirt. "You're slipping, Mom. Why didn't you remind me for the tenth time that he hasn't got a penny to bless himself with?"

Nora's hands paused in their buttoning of Drew's pajama top. She cast her daughter an odd look, then continued fastening buttons. "If he had a million dollars, it wouldn't make any difference to how I feel. He's not the right man for you, Lindy Beth. He's wild, and . . . and . . ."

"Sexy?" Linda supplied.

Nora blushed angrily. "Handsome is as handsome does. You need another husband like Jim. Somebody who's steady and reliable. You don't want a husband who's . . . who's . . . what you said."

It was as if she had been struck by the proverbial flash of lightning. "But I do want a man like Matt," Linda protested softly. "I've just realized that's *exactly* what I do want. I want somebody who makes me feel *alive*, somebody who makes me feel like a woman. I want Matt. I love him, Mom. I always have."

Nora's cheeks burned brick red. "Bedtime, children," she said sharply. "Off you go! Your grandad's waiting to read you a story. Remember, you have to be up early tomorrow. It's the Sunday school social, and we're going on a picnic."

"Wait!" Linda caught the twins as they scampered past, gathering them into a bear hug. "Hey, kids, before you go to sleep, there's something I want to tell you. I won't be going on the picnic with you tomorrow. Will you be extra good for Granny and Grandad, please?"

"Why aren't you coming?" Kate demanded.

"Matt's a very old friend of mine, and I'd like to spend a few hours alone with him. We have some— talking to do."

"You talked to him already, lots of times." Drew sounded accusing.

"Yes, I know, but he works in New York, which is a long way from here, and we may not have a chance to see each other again for a while."

"Okay. Have a nice time," Drew said politely. He seemed to have entirely forgotten his earlier concern about being abandoned. As for Kate, she was already wriggling out of Linda's hug, obviously bored by the subject of her mother's plans. "I want Grandad to read us *Green Eggs and Ham*," she said.

"You always choose that book," Drew complained. "I want *The King, the Mice, and the Cheese*."

Linda ushered them into their bedroom, where her father was already waiting. "Maybe if you ask Grandad very nicely, he'll read you both stories," she suggested. "I'll come upstairs and say good night to you both in a minute."

Nora had finished tidying the bathroom and was waiting for Linda at the head of the stairs. "I'll have a private word with you in the kitchen, if you don't mind." Without waiting for an answer, she pivoted on her heel and marched down the stairs.

"Don't you have a grain of sense left in that head of yours?" she demanded as soon as they reached the kitchen. "Matt Deighton proved what kind of a man he was seven years ago, when he left Suzanne Mackenzie in the lurch—"

"I agree Matt proved what kind of a man he was seven years ago. He proved that he was too kindhearted for his own good. Suzanne made a few wild statements when she was half out of her mind with panic, and the town of Carson picked up on them as if they were rock-hard facts. Everybody wanted Matt to be the villain. He'd thumbed his nose at Carson one time too often, and all our upright citizens were circling like sharks, waiting to move in for the kill."

"You've always tried to pretend he was innocent."

"I had the best reason for knowing he wasn't with Suzanne the night all the fuss started."

"Her dad came home and saw Matthew climbing out of the bedroom window."

"No, he didn't. Her dad came home and saw *somebody* climbing out of the window. Coach Mackenzie chose to accuse Matt." Linda drew in a deep breath. "You may as well know the truth, Mom, because I think you've suspected it for years. Matt was with me that night, all night long. He couldn't have been anywhere near Suzanne Mackenzie."

Nora paled, fussing with the dishcloth in order to

have somewhere to look other than at Linda's eyes. "If he was with you, why didn't he say anything when the police started making their inquiries?"

"Partly because he was protecting me, and partly, I think, he hoped I'd find the courage to admit the truth myself. And besides that, he was protecting another family in town. You see, Matt knew all along who the real father of Suzanne's baby was."

"Wh-who was it?"

"Mr. Beckworth, the high school principal. But Beckworth was married with three children, and Matt didn't want to point any accusing fingers. He simply went to the principal, told him what he knew, and asked him to resign."

"The high school principal?" Nora wrung out the dishcloth and wiped the already immaculate draining board. "It's true, Beckworth did move out of town. About a week before Matt, wasn't it?"

"I don't remember. I wasn't paying any attention at the time."

Nora removed a platter of chicken salad from the fridge. "He's still not going to marry you, Lindy Beth."

"I know," she said quietly. "That bothers me, Mom, I admit it. One day, I'd like very much to be happily married. But I'm beginning to realize that sometimes people should settle for less than their ideal. I love Matt, Mom, and I'm prepared to take whatever part of him he's willing to give me."

"When I was a young girl, I'd never have dreamed of saying something so immoral to my mother."

"When I was a young girl, I wouldn't have said it, either. Mom, I'm a woman now, not a girl."

Nora sniffed. "I suppose you'll threaten to take the children over to that miserable Sally Deighton woman if I refuse to take care of them."

"No. Except in an emergency, I think the twins are too young to be left overnight with anybody except you and Dad. So if you don't want me to spend the weekend with Matt, all you have to do is refuse to look after the children. You can stop me from going to Grand Junction if you want to. You have complete control."

Nora banged the chicken salad down onto the kitchen table, not even stopping to wipe up a shred of lettuce leaf that bounced off the platter. "You could at least pretend you're not planning to . . . to sleep with him."

"Why? We both know that I am."

"That you are what?" Ron Owen asked, walking into the kitchen. "My, that salad looks good, Nora-love."

"Linda's going to spend the weekend with Matthew Deighton in Grand Junction." The words spilled out of Nora in an agitated rush.

Her father looked at Linda consideringly. "You sure you know what you're up to, lass?"

"I've never been more sure of anything."

Ron looked across at his wife. "Does she know about him?" he asked. "Did you tell her what Mrs. Wittmeyer found out?"

Linda gave an exasperated sigh. "Dad, please don't. There is absolutely nothing that Mrs. Wittmeyer has to say about Matt that I want to hear."

"No, I didn't tell her," Nora said. She glanced meaningfully at her husband. "I think it's better if she doesn't know."

"Whatever you say, love," Ron agreed doubtfully. "When are you leaving, Lindy Beth?"

"As soon as I can pack a bag and say good night to the twins," she said, thrusting her parents' heavy-handed hints out of her mind. Whatever scandalous nugget Greta Wittmeyer had dug up, it couldn't be anything *too* terrible, or Nora would have been rushing to repeat it. She gave her father a quick hug. "Enjoy your dinner, Dad. I'll look in to say good-bye." She hesitated for a split second, then dropped a kiss on Nora's scrubbed, wrinkled cheek. "Take care, Mom, and thank you for looking after the children. I'll call tomorrow, and I'll be back on Sunday evening."

Nora turned away, her narrow shoulders hunched, her voice thick with embarrassment. "I love you, Lindy Beth. You know that, don't you?"

Linda rested her cheek against her mother's face. "Yes, Mom, I've always known it. I love you and Dad, too."

Ron Owen cleared his throat. "Before we drown the salad in tears, do you think we could start dinner?"

Chapter Nine

THE SUN DISAPPEARED in a blaze of purple-and-orange glory behind the mountains. Matt turned his steak on the barbecue and stared unseeingly toward the cascade of water that marked the grotto end of Doug Hotchkiss's swimming pool. He rubbed his forehead, easing the ache of fatigue and tension. Given that he'd just put in an exceptionally successful day's work on the set mockups for *American Eagle*, he wasn't feeling too pleased with himself.

He took a sip of his beer, closing his eyes as the ice-cold brew momentarily numbed his throat. Smoke teased his nostrils with the appetizing smell of sizzled barbecue sauce. He prodded his steak with a fork. Almost ready. He brought his plate over to the grill and unwrapped the foil from an ear of fresh corn and a baked potato. The single servings looked lost on the vastness of the oversized grill.

Frowning, Matt plunked the steak onto a vacant patch of plate, then slathered his potato in sour cream. To hell with cholesterol, and doctors who believed everybody should live on grilled fish and steamed asparagus. Right at this moment, it didn't seem worth seventy-two years of abstinence so he could celebrate his hundredth birthday with a slice of chocolate cake.

If only Linda were here, the night wouldn't feel so

empty. Matt accepted that thought reluctantly, but without surprise. Generally, when he worked he couldn't stand being around people, but Linda was different and always had been. He found her presence warming rather than intrusive, soothing rather than irritating.

A vivid image of her passion-slick body arched to receive him flashed into Matt's mind, and he grimaced wryly. Whom was he kidding? He didn't miss Linda because she was quiet and soothing. He missed her because he desired her. Because he loved her.

He put his plate down on the wooden table and swore silently. He hadn't planned on letting that particular thought take shape in his mind. He wasn't ready to be in love, and especially not with Linda.

A teasing voice spoke out of the darkness. "If you're not gonna eat that dinner, mister, you could pass it in my direction. I'm starving."

For an instant, Matt wondered if he'd summoned Linda's voice from out of the depths of his fantasies. Slowly, he turned around.

It was no fantasy. She was real all right—achingly, gloriously real. Half-smiling, half-questioning, she leaned against one of the wooden patio pillars, her stance blatantly provocative. The evening breeze ruffled her hair and molded the thin muslin of her dress against her thighs. The glow from the overhead lantern bathed her skin in a soft radiance and lit her hair with silver highlights. Matt had never seen a woman who looked more beautiful. He had never wanted a woman more.

"You're awful quiet, mister. I can...I could go away, if you don't want company."

Matt's gaze locked with hers. "I want *your* company."

"Your food's getting cold, mister. It's a shame to waste it. May I share it with you?"

His eyes gleamed as he pulled his dinner plate back toward him. He rocked his chair onto its hind legs, feeling his desire mingle with an irrepressible bubble of happiness, a happiness he didn't attempt to analyze. When he answered Linda, he mimicked her exaggerated western drawl. "The food in this establishment comes kind of expensive, little lady."

The wind blew a strand of golden hair across her mouth, and Matt watched, mesmerized, as she slowly brushed it away. "I can pay," she said.

"You sure do look—hungry."

"I am, mister. I'm *real* hungry."

Matt reminded himself to breathe. He cut a mouthful of steak and chewed it as though he savored every morsel. In fact, he might just as well have been chewing wood pulp. "Folks who know me'll tell you I've got a roarin' appetite, little lady. I reckon your appetite wouldn't even begin to stack up alongside of mine."

"You might be surprised, mister," she said huskily. "I haven't had nothin' for two days, and I'm willin' to pay a high price for my supper."

He stroked his chin. "Well, now, little lady, this is prime cookin' we're talkin' about. I've gotta warn you, there's lots of ladies anxious for a taste of my home cookin'."

Linda's eyes held a wealth of promise. "I heard you serve wonderful . . . meals, mister. I'll give you a fair price, more than fair."

Matt's body grew hard. He was tempted just to drag her into his arms and kiss her senseless, but he didn't want to stop their game. The undulating sway of her hips each time she spoke was a highly pleasurable form of torture. "That's all very well, lady, but steak's only the start of this dinner. Did you notice the baked potato and fresh-grown corn? This is what you might call a high-quality meal, and it's gonna cost you dear."

She nodded solemnly, although her voice quivered with laughter. "Name your price, mister. I'm desperate. Like I said, I've spent two days and two whole nights in the desert. I'll do anything for—food."

Matt lowered his glass. The beer foam clung to his mouth, and he wiped it away with the back of his hand. "Then here's my price, lady. The cost for this food is one item of clothing per bite. Use of my knife and fork comes free."

He could actually see the little shudder of awareness that rippled through her body. "You drive an awful hard bargain," she murmured. "But folks who've been wandering in the desert are too hungry to care, I reckon. I'll pay what you ask, mister."

"Then start undressing."

She bent over and slowly unbuckled the strap of her sandal. The laughter faded from her eyes as she held the shoe out to him.

"Bring it here," he commanded roughly.

She limped over and stood in front of him. "Is this what you wanted, mister?"

"It's a start," he said hoarsely, taking the white sandal and putting it carefully on the bench beside him. He offered her a forkful of potato. "You'll find other items of clothing bring bigger rewards."

"Potato's fine," she said, eating with exaggerated pleasure. She handed back the fork, and he caressed her fingers, unable to resist touching her. She clutched her hands to her bosom in mock dismay.

"Oh, no, mister! You wouldn't be planning on taking advantage of a poor little lady lost in the desert, would you?"

"You bet your sweet petunias I'm planning on taking advantage," he muttered.

She fluttered her lashes. "Just because I'm willing to take off my clothes, mister, doesn't mean that I'm *forward.*"

"Forward, backward. Lady, keep wiggling your tush like that, and it won't make any difference to me."

Linda bit back a gurgle of laughter. "Mister, you're very crude."

"Lady, you're very sexy."

The sound of the cicadas seemed loud as Linda slowly unbuckled her other sandal. This time Matt rewarded her with a piece of steak and her own can of beer.

"Thanks, mister." Linda popped the cap on the beer, and took a long swallow. Her fingers sought out the top button at the front of her dress, then paused tantalizingly. "Seems like this old button is stuck," she whispered. "Want to help me out, mister?"

"Reckon I might." He stood up, aware that his hand was shaking as he reached for the button Linda had indicated. By the time the final fastening at her waist had been undone, he was hot and aching with need.

She pushed the dress off her shoulders, revealing a transparent bra of peach-colored lace. She wiggled her hips slightly, and the dress slid over the flatness of her stomach to settle in a pale blue pool at her feet.

Matt took one look at the perfection of her body and gave up the game in a hurry. "No more," he said, taking her lips in an urgent kiss. "My God, Linda, no more. You'll drive me crazy."

She moved in sinuous protest. "But, mister, I'm still hungry."

"I'll take care of your hunger," he murmured. "Like this."

He could feel the intensity of her response as he moved

his mouth over hers in a long, seeking kiss. When the last edge of her resistance vanished, he lifted her into his arms and walked down the stone-flagged path to the pool. "Did you sleep last night?" he asked softly.

She shook her head.

"Neither did I. Every time I closed my eyes, all I could see was the two of us making love." He lowered her onto an air mattress beside the pool, and she gasped as the night-chilled plastic touched her bare skin. "Cold?" he asked.

"A bit."

"I'll make you warm again," he promised, following her down onto the mattress. "I'm sorry. I wasn't sure I'd make it as far as the bedroom."

He took her into his arms, covering her with his body, his hands tangling mindlessly in her hair. Her breasts felt soft against his chest, her skin delicate and smooth against his. He wanted this moment of anticipation to last forever—he wanted to take her right that second, to explode into her with all the force of his pent-up passion.

Matt kissed her mouth, her breasts, her stomach. He shaped her body with his hands, trying to make her feel all the heat and desire and hunger behind his lovemaking. Her breath began to come in short, sharp little pants of pleasure, and he pulled her against him, cradling his hips in the sheltering circle of her thighs. God, but making love had never felt like this before. Never this burning, aching urgency to join himself with another human being and share her sensations.

She reached for the zipper of his jeans. "Take them off, Matt," she whispered, her words scarcely audible. "I want to feel you against me."

Somehow—he wasn't at all sure how—he managed to stand up and tear off his jeans and shorts. Thank God he hadn't been wearing anything else! He knelt beside Linda, removing her bra and panties with little more finesse than he'd displayed in ripping off his jeans. In a single swift movement, he straddled her, his penetration hard and deep.

"Ah, Matt! You keep . . . making me . . . hungrier."

Her face was flushed with desire, damp with sweat, taut with longing—and he wanted her as he'd never .ited a woman before. He had to clench his teeth to keep from thrusting into her and finishing it all with a single stroke. Straining for willpower, he held himself back. There had been almost no traditional foreplay between the two of them, and he couldn't believe Linda was as aroused as he. But as soon as he began to move, she responded, lifting her hips eagerly to meet his strokes.

She clasped her hands behind his neck, holding him to her. Shuddering, her body melted into his. "Matt, I love you."

He wasn't sure whether he heard the words or whether he simply absorbed them, drawing them out of her quivering body and into his own. He relaxed his control and allowed the final surge of passion to overwhelm them. "I love you, too, Linda."

For a few ecstatic moments, the world ceased to exist.

They swam in the night-black waters of the pool while the reheated barbecue coals broiled another two steaks and two more ears of corn. It was nearly midnight when their meal was finally ready, but the temperature was still a comfortable seventy, and they chose to eat outside on the patio.

"No bugs," Linda said, leaning back in her chair, replete with food and happiness. "That's one of the best things about Colorado."

Matt grinned. "Mmm. Rattlesnakes and killer bees are so much nicer to have around than chiggers or mosquitoes."

She pulled a face. "At least you can see them more easily!"

"True." Matt leaned across the table and took her hand into his. "Marry me, Linda," he said simply.

She felt her entire being go still. As soon as she started breathing again, a hundred practical objections flew into her mind. She ignored them all. She had married once for sound, practical reasons, and it had been a disaster. This time, she would be smart enough to marry for love. Blood pumped thickly through her veins as she looked down at his hand, curved possessively over hers. "Yes," she said. "Oh, yes, please, Matt. That would be wonderful."

He carried her hand to his mouth, and pressed a kiss into her palm. "I love you, Linda."

"I love you, too, Matt. I think I've loved you all my life."

"Your parents are going to be upset."

"I'm not eighteen anymore, Matt."

"I expect you're worried about living in New York with the twins—"

"I'm not," she said quickly. "I realize we can find lots of solutions if we really work at our problems. There must be a million families who have homes in the suburbs around the city. We'll find a house we can afford somewhere within commuting range of your work."

"My work at the construction company, you mean?" He seemed amused.

"Yes." She perched on his lap, nestling her head against his chest. "And when that project is finished, you'll get another one, I just know it. And there's always the income from my Rumbles contract to fall back on."

He kissed her tenderly on the end of her nose. "Not to mention my paintings. Remember? I'm about to become a famous artist."

"Yes." At that precise moment, she almost believed it. At this moment, anything seemed possible, even that Matt should break into the incredibly competitive world of commercial art. Lord knew, he had the talent. She giggled, dizzy with joyful anticipation. "Soon you'll be rich and famous, and I'll have to post a guard to keep all the women away from you."

He frowned with mock-ferocity. "Watch it, woman, you're stepping on my masculine ego."

Realization dawned, and she laughed. "Oh, I'm sorry! Of course, I'm sure *hundreds* of women already desire you! Since we can't afford to post a guard, I'll have to fight personally to keep them all away."

"You won't have to fight very hard. You have an unbeatable weapon."

She looked at him quizzically.

"When you're around, I can't see any other woman," he admitted, his voice husky.

Linda felt warm with love as she wrapped her arms around him. "It feels so right, doesn't it, Matt? As if we've finally come to our senses after seven years of being complete fools."

He kissed the top of her head. "It feels good," he agreed.

Sleepily, Linda curled deeper into his arms. "Why didn't you ever come back to Carson, Matt?"

"Why didn't you come to New York?" he countered.

"I was afraid. Of my parents. Of Carson. Of myself."

He looked into the distance. "I guess I was afraid, too."

"Afraid? *You?* But what of?"

"Of not making it in New York. And then of you

and Jim Petrie. Of seeing you with him and discovering that you really did love him more than me."

"I never loved Jim."

Her words hung in the darkness, pulsing between them. Matt spoke softly. "I was crazy with jealousy when my mom wrote to say you'd gotten engaged, and I was tempted to call and tell you what a fool you were being. But then I realized I had no right."

"I think I knew anyway. That I was being a fool, I mean. But everybody liked Jim, and he felt so—safe."

"It'll never be safe or easy for us—you know that, don't you, Linda?"

"I guess safe isn't what I want anymore."

He lifted her up and twisted her around so that she straddled him on the chair. His arms tightened around her waist, holding her so close that she could feel the hardness of his arousal and the urgency of his need. Her own desire reignited with sudden, shocking intensity— shocking because she had thought she was too sleepy to respond to even the most skilled lovemaking.

His voice was low, almost gruff, in her ear. "That's how it is when I'm near you, Lindy Beth. That's the way it's always been."

She tilted her head back, parting her robe, offering herself to him. "That's the way it is for me too, Matt."

Sally and Frank Deighton were sitting on the Owens' back porch drinking iced tea when Matt and Linda arrived home from Grand Junction on Sunday evening. Greta Wittmeyer, with her remarkable capacity for always being in the right place to hear Carson's latest gossip, was with them. Perched on the edge of her chair, a hungry starling ready to grab any morsel of scandal, she bided her time with foot-tapping impatience as Matt and Linda greeted their parents and inquired about the twins. Mrs. Wittmeyer's supersensitive antennae were all shouting that this was going to be a Big Night for News.

"The twins are in bed," Nora informed her daughter, with more than a touch of disapproval. "You know I don't believe in keeping children up after their bedtime, and it's eight-thirty already."

"I'm sorry. We—um—we got delayed at the last minute." Linda lobbed a glance of desperate appeal in Matt's direction. She was hopeless at this sort of social deception.

He gave her a reassuring grin. "An emergency rescue," he drawled, putting his arm around her shoulders. "But Linda managed to take care of it for us."

Linda could feel herself turning scarlet under Mrs. Wittmeyer's fascinated scrutiny. She braced herself for one of that lady's withering comments, but it never came.

"The pair of you seem to have been enjoying yourselves over the weekend," Mrs. Wittmeyer simpered.

"We have." Matt's gaze flicked from Linda to his parents and back again. "We were celebrating."

Nora gasped, Ron Owen stirred uneasily, and Sally and Frank Deighton exchanged swift glances. Before anybody else could speak, Mrs. Wittmeyer rushed into the fray. "And I'm sure you both have every reason to celebrate. You were a wise man, Matthew, to come back to your hometown when you finally decided to settle down. And our sweet little Lindy Beth is just the right girl for you."

Linda stared at Mrs. Wittmeyer, puzzled by her gushing manner. Weddings were one of that lady's favorite topics, but they weren't usually cause for outpourings of coy goodwill. From Greta Wittmeyer's point of view, the most satisfactory impending marriages were always ones where she could prophesy di-

saster. It was entirely out of character for her to be smiling so sweetly at Matt when she ought to have been
needling him with questions about how he planned to
support a wife and two children without a steady job or
an assured income. Come to that, why was Mrs. Wittmeyer being generous enough to assume Linda and Matt
would be married? Matt hadn't actually said they were
engaged, and Mrs. Wittmeyer never gave people the
benefit of the doubt if she could avoid it.

"Nothing's settled yet," Linda said hastily. The last
thing she wanted to do was discuss wedding plans with
her parents and the Deightons while Mrs. Wittmeyer sat
by. She and Matt hadn't begun to work out the practical
problems connected with their marriage, and Mrs. Wittmeyer's comments—even her strangely gushing ones
—weren't likely to help in finding workable solutions.

"Well, dear, you don't want to let things drag out, do
you?" Mrs. Wittmeyer's smile suddenly contained its
usual poisonous undertones. "I mean, we have to be
practical about marriage these days, don't we? And a
man like Matthew doesn't come along more than once
in a girl's lifetime. You're a naughty little puss for holding out on me when you had such exciting news about
one of Carson's hometown boys. Fortunately, I have a
cousin in New York who filled me in on Matthew's
wonderful success story."

Linda stared at Mrs. Wittmeyer in blank bewilderment. What in the world was the woman talking about?
Why was she suddenly transforming Matt from Carson's
official ne'er-do-well into a favored *hometown boy* with
a "wonderful success story" to his credit?

Frank Deighton spoke into the curiously tense silence. "Matt's professional name is Grant Deighton. I
thought you knew, Linda." His voice took on an acid
tinge. "I thought everybody in Carson knew. Seems to

me, Greta spent last Friday spreading the news through the entire western slope of the Rockies."

Linda took in only the first part of Frank's statement. "Grant Deighton?" she repeated blankly. She pivoted, turning from the sympathetic faces of the Deightons to the guilty faces of her parents, and finally to Matt. "You're *Grant Deighton?* You designed all the sets for *Legend of the Witch* and never told me?"

The look he gave her was withering in its contempt. "No, I never told you. But I guess very recently someone else did."

Linda was still taking in only about one word in three that anyone said. Hurt, puzzled, she looked at her mother. "You and Dad knew about this?"

"Only on Saturday," Nora said stiffly.

Sally Deighton tried to smooth over a situation that was becoming uncomfortable for everybody, except Greta Wittmeyer, whose nose was twitching faster and faster with excitement. "I guess you're the only person in Carson who *didn't* know, Linda," Sally said. Ignoring Matt's skeptical snort, she went on, "Why are you looking so shocked, honey? It's good news, isn't it? I would have told you years ago, but Matt had this obsession about not letting people in Carson know how successful he'd been. You know how he is. I think he found it amusing, the way everybody assumed he'd made a total mess of his life."

"I guess so." Linda wasn't even sure herself why she found the information so shattering. The knowledge that Matt was successful, famous, and undoubtedly rich ought to have made her decision to marry him seem all the more right. Instead, she was filled with a sense of foreboding.

She looked again at Matt. She couldn't understand why, but he still appeared angry—and with her, not Greta Wittmeyer, who was surely the logical person to get mad at.

"Would you all excuse us for a minute?" he said. "Linda and I need to talk." He stormed into the kitchen without waiting for anybody's response and, after a moment's hesitation, Linda followed him.

He turned on her the minute she shut the screen door. "God, I'm such a fool! You did it again, didn't you, Linda?"

"Did what?" she asked, still not able to connect the cutting fury of his manner to anything personal in their relationship.

"Oh, come on, Lindy Beth! I've known you for twenty-five years. I know why you suddenly turned up in Grand Junction yesterday."

Linda felt cold all the way to her heart. "What are you saying, Matt? Why are you so angry?"

"I guess I'm just like any other guy. I'm not wild about being married for my money."

"And that's what you think I'm doing?"

"Isn't it obvious?" he asked bitterly. "On Thursday, I was plain old Matt Deighton, and there was no way I could persuade you to spend any time with me. *It wouldn't be right. There were the twins to think of. We had to consider the future.* On Saturday, you discover I'm Grant Deighton, millionaire, and hey, presto! You're right there with me in Doug Hotchkiss's backyard and you're putting out for me in a way I never dreamed you could put out. But I don't need that sort of sex, honey. I can find it cheaper and a hell of a lot less complicated back home in New York."

Linda stared at him, totally appalled. "Matt, you're wrong! I didn't know anything about your career. I was working all day—"

"Honey, that look of hurt innocence is real nice, but right now, I'm not in the mood to be convinced. Try me later, when I need the sex more."

Linda closed her eyes, shutting out the image of Matt's cruel expression. "I was working on patterns for the Rumbles' clothes," she said desperately. "Matt, I didn't talk to anybody on Friday *or* Saturday. I didn't know anything about your darn career when I came to Grand Junction!"

"Your parents knew, and despite the little charade a few minutes ago, I can't believe they wouldn't tell you. Why would they keep information like that a secret?"

Linda's temper snapped. Indifferent to the interested silence on the porch, where all five people had long since abandoned any pretense of maintaining their own conversation, she yelled her answer. "Why didn't they tell me? I guess because they have the same low opinion of my morals you do. They obviously thought that one word about how much money you had and what a famous artist you were, and I'd be tearing off to Grand Junction, throwing myself into your arms, hoping to squeeze an offer of marriage out of you. Well, they only got the equation half right. I *did* go tearing off to Grand Junction, and I *did* throw myself into your arms, but it had nothing to do with money or security, or wanting to marry a millionaire. It was because I *loved* you, dammit! Because for once in my life I was prepared to do something and say to heck with the consequences! To heck with what people think!"

She stopped yelling only because she had run out of air and had to stop to draw breath. Looking stricken, Matt reached out his hand. "Linda, I'm sorry. I jumped to conclusions—"

She snatched her hand away. "You're darn right, you jumped to conclusions, Matthew Deighton!" Her temper hadn't even cooled, let alone dissipated. "Everybody in this whole darn town is forever jumping to conclusions about me, and they're usually wrong! I'm not perfect!

I'm not sweet! I'm not a mindless moron! I'm as crazy and mixed up as anybody else, but at least I've managed to get something straight! I know that the only thing worse than a marriage without love is a marriage without trust. And you obviously don't trust me, Matt. You didn't trust me enough to tell me the truth about your career, and you didn't trust me enough to believe that I wouldn't—couldn't—marry you just because you're rich and famous."

"Maybe it was myself I didn't trust," Matt said quietly. "Linda, if you knew how many women had offered to make love to me as part of their career-enhancement projects, you might understand why I jumped to conclusions."

"But they're women in general," Linda said, the temper seeping out of her, leaving her sad and deflated. "I'm me. After that night in Denver, I thought we knew one another, trusted each other with some of our most intimate secrets. Now I find out that I didn't have any idea who you were or what you'd achieved. You lied to me, Matt."

"No," he denied quickly. "Never that. I just didn't tell you the whole truth."

"But why not? Why ever in the world not?"

"Because I wanted you to ask me point-blank what had happened to my career ambitions," he said finally. "Dammit, Linda, we spent that entire summer after you graduated from high school talking about what I planned to do in New York, how I planned to build my career. Did you have so little faith in my talent that you really thought I'd come back to Carson broke and scratching for a job?"

"And did you have so little faith in my integrity that you actually believed I'd marry you for your money?"

"I've apologized," he said stiffly. "Linda, it was all a silly misunderstanding."

"We made a mistake, Matt, and we ought to admit it now, before it's too late. We have a sexual attraction that's strong enough to blind us to the fundamentals. Sex isn't enough to make a marriage."

"It feels like a pretty damn good basis to me."

She smiled sadly. "And to me. That's what makes it so tough to say good-bye."

" 'Here's looking at you, kid,' and a cut to the sunset only works in the movies. Don't do this to us, Linda."

"I have to." She touched his mouth with the lightest, most fleeting of kisses. "Good-bye, Matt." Ignoring his urgent murmur of her name, she ran upstairs and locked herself in her bedroom.

Matt stared after her for several silent seconds, then strode angrily out of the kitchen onto the porch. The banging of the door roused the five listeners to instant action.

Greta Wittmeyer was the first to move—naturally, since it was ten o'clock already, and she had a packed schedule of phone calls to make within the next hour. She made a hasty round of good-byes, and dashed off down the garden path, totally ignored by everyone.

Matt thrust his hand into the pocket of his jeans. "I guess you heard what happened."

"You weren't exactly whispering," Sally replied. Surprisingly, she sounded amused.

"It wouldn't have worked out," Nora said to nobody in particular. "The two of them aren't suited for each other in the least. It's just as well that they had their disagreement now."

Ron Owen forced his wife to meet his eyes. "Matt and Linda are perfect for each other," he contradicted gently. "What's more, we've both known that for years."

Nora's reply was anguished. "But Lindy Beth doesn't want to marry him. She said so herself!"

"You wouldn't be so upset if you thought Linda meant what she said." Sally Deighton patted Nora's shoulder. "Things'll work out, you'll see. If the pair of them haven't got the sense to sort themselves out, we'll have to do the sorting for them."

Matt groaned and looked at his mother, his expression half-hopeful, half-wary. "What outrageous scheme are you cooking up now, Mom?"

"Matt, my boy, a wise man doesn't ask. When Sally gets that gleam in her eyes, the rest of us had better watch out." Frank Deighton stood up and brushed off his baggy pants. He grinned at Matt. "I'll tell you one thing: Your mother'll have the wedding date fixed within the week, I guarantee it."

Sally gazed into the distance. "A double wedding," she murmured. "Jennifer and Doug. Matt and Linda. What do you think, Frank? In the garden, before the weather turns cold."

"Now, love, you know we shouldn't interfere in our children's lives. Matt and Linda are quite old enough to make their own decisions." He puffed on his pipe and gave Ron an exaggerated wink. "How's that for the masterful male, huh? Don't you think I've got the technique down pat?"

Ron laughed. "I'll tell you what I think, Frank. I think we'd better start planning a double wedding."

Chapter Ten

As SOON AS she woke up the next morning, Linda discovered an urgent need to buy the twins new sneakers. By taking off for the local shopping mall right after breakfast, she managed to escape from the house without speaking to either of her parents—or to anybody else who might come looking for her.

She returned home at lunchtime, determined not to see Matt, and equally determined to avoid rehashing the events of the previous night with Nora. She had spent the car journey home reminding herself that she was an adult woman, and for once she was going to be firm about her right to privacy. She wouldn't listen to her mother's inevitable lecture on the folly of becoming involved with a man like Matthew Deighton. She'd already given herself more than enough versions of the same lecture.

Nora, however, showed no desire to discuss Matthew Deighton. She greeted Linda with a bland smile. "Hello, dear. Any luck in finding shoes for the twins?"

"I gottened pink ones," Kate said, triumphantly holding up a pair of bright yellow sneakers. She was learning her colors, but so far the subtleties of the shade pink had eluded her.

"I gottened red." Drew opened his box and showed Nora his new shoes.

"Very nice, dears." Nora took the children over to the sink and helped them wash their hands. "I've made you peanut-butter-and-banana sandwiches for lunch."

The twins expressed suitable rapture, and Linda set out some paper napkins and two mugs of milk. She waited for her mother to start asking her usual probing questions. None were forthcoming. Nora seemed to have suffered total amnesia as far as the events of the previous night were concerned. Linda found the situation very disconcerting. She was all ready to stand up for her rights—except nobody seemed interested in fighting.

"Any messages for me?" she asked airily, when it became apparent not only that Nora had no intention of delivering a lecture about Matt, but that she didn't even plan to mention his name.

"Messages?" Nora asked vaguely. "What sort of messages?"

"Oh, I don't know. Maybe a phone call or something."

Nora's glance held an infuriating trace of sympathy. "No, dear, I'm afraid not."

"It doesn't matter. I wasn't expecting anything important."

"Right, dear. That must be why nobody called. What are you planning to do this afternoon while the children nap?"

Crawl into a deep hole and slash my wrists. Or, alternatively, call Matt.

Linda hastily pushed away the treacherous thought. Last night, she'd told Matt she wouldn't marry him in the heat of anger, but she was absolutely, positively certain that she'd made the correct decision. A relationship based on half-truths and misunderstandings didn't have a chance of long-term success.

"I thought I might get my hair cut," she said, answering her mother. "It needs trimming."

"That's a good idea," Nora agreed placidly. "And there's a Disney movie on TV tonight. We can all watch it together."

"Wonderful," Linda said, her voice hollow. She wiped milk from Kate's mouth and peanut butter from Drew's fingers. Of course it was much better that Matt hadn't come pounding on the door, demanding to see her, arrogantly insisting that she should change her mind. But it would have been nice if he'd exerted just the *tiniest* bit of pressure to persuade her to marry him. After all, people sometimes said things in the midst of an argument that they didn't entirely mean, and she and Matt had seven years of separation to overcome, and trust could grow between people if you worked at it—

Linda snapped off her train of dangerously wishful thinking. What she and Matt shared was nothing more than a powerful sexual attraction. And a bunch of fond memories. And a deep interest in commercial art, and . . . Linda's thoughts skittered to another feverish halt. Art. The Rumbles. Her contract with Playbrite. Oh, dear God! Her contract with Playbrite!

She whirled around. "Mom, what position does Matthew hold with the Playbrite Toy Company?"

"I think Greta said he was a director or some such thing. He and the president—Charlie, isn't that his name?—met up when Matt first went to New York. Now that Matt's so famous, and won so many awards for his art, lots of companies like to have him on their board as a sort of design consultant . . ."

Nora's final words were delivered to her daughter's retreating back, as Linda tore up the stairs and into her room. Once there, she scrabbled frantically through the papers of her desk until she found her copy of the preliminary contract with Playbrite. She flung herself onto the bed and stared at the typewritten pages with tear-filled eyes. What a conceited fool she'd been! How could she possibly have imagined the Rumbles were really good enough to command a fabulous advance like ten thousand dollars? Matt had just been humoring her. With all the power he wielded on the Playbrite board, he could undoubtedly call in a favor now and then. Nobody at Playbrite really thought her designs were any good. The company would churn out a few dozen Rumbles, and that would probably be the last anybody ever heard of them.

Linda walked over to her drawing board and flipped through the illustrations for the storybook she'd envisaged. Her critical eye spotted a hundred amateurish defects that she hadn't noticed in her creative euphoria Friday night. Her cheeks flamed. It was positively embarrassing to think she'd almost sent these drawings off to New York with a suggestion that Playbrite might like to use them.

She reached out, intending to tear the illustrations to shreds, but something stayed her hand. Instead, she took the contract and tore it into a dozen small pieces. She shoved the pieces inside an envelope and added a note.

Matt, thanks for your charitable impulse, but I don't need the money that badly.

She signed her name with a flourish, and stalked downstairs.

Nora peered around the kitchen door. "Off to have your hair cut, dear?"

"Not right now. I have something to give Matt."

"If you hurry, you may catch him. I believe he's leaving for New York this afternoon."

Linda stared at her mother as if she'd grown two heads. "Matt's leaving? This afternoon?"

"I think so, dear. You'd better hurry if you want to catch him. I'll put the twins down for their nap while you're gone."

Once again, Nora was talking to her daughter's back.

Sally Deighton greeted Linda with the same infuriating sort of sympathetic smile that Nora had been producing all morning. "Hello, Linda. What can I do for you, dear?"

"I . . . er . . . I had something to give to Matt."

"Do you need to see him personally, dear? He's in rather a hurry to catch his plane. I doubt if he has time . . ."

Linda wasn't sure whether to burst into tears or yell with frustration. She compromised by drawing herself up in a passable imitation of icy dignity. "I wouldn't want to interrupt Matt when he's so busy. But perhaps you'd make sure that he gets this envelope before he leaves?"

"Certainly, dear." Sally Deighton took the package and tucked it absentmindedly under her arm. "And how are the twins this morning?"

"Very well, thank you."

"Good. You must all set aside next- Saturday, the twins as well. We're having a special party. Don't breathe a word to a soul, but Jennifer and Doug are going to announce their engagement."

"Oh, Sally, that's terrific!" For a moment, Linda forgot her own misery in a rush of happiness for her friend. "May I tell my parents?"

"They already know. They were over here this morning when Jennifer called us."

"They were over here? Dad as well? Why wasn't he at work?"

Sally looked a little flustered. "I don't know, Linda. He only stopped by for a few minutes anyway. Oh, will you listen to that? I can hear a pot boiling over on my stove. I must run. Bye, dear. See you Saturday!" Sally shut the door with a decisive click.

Linda wandered home, wondering why she had an insane desire to see Matt face-to-face, just so that she could inform him that she was absolutely, positively certain that her decision not to marry him was correct. Lord knew, there wasn't much need to keep reiterating her position. Matt didn't seem to have the slightest interest in trying to make her change her mind.

Linda sniffed, repressing the impulse to burst into tears of self-pity. Why was she feeling so miserable? She was the one who'd made the decision not to marry Matt. Last night had proved once and for all that they were hopelessly unsuited. She was furious with him for not telling her the truth about his career, and even more furious with him for leaping to the conclusion that she was marrying him for his money. Just because the sex between them was incandescent—

The doorbell rang. Her heart stopped beating for a split second, then raced forward at twice its normal speed. She dashed back into the hallway and pulled open the door.

Sally Deighton waited on the doorstep. She smiled. "Hello again, dear. Matt just left, but he asked me to give you this." Sally handed over a brown envelope.

With trembling fingers, Linda ripped open the flap. Pieces of her Playbrite contract fluttered to the floor, together with a note.

> *Linda, hope you have either plenty of sticky tape or plenty of spare cash. Playbrite is a for-profit company, not a charitable organization.*

They bought your Rumbles designs because they were good. They'll sue the pants off you if you don't live up to your contract terms. Here's looking at you, kid. Matt.

"You seem upset, dear." Sally's voice was infuriatingly soothing. "I hope Matt didn't say anything to annoy you?"

Linda shook her head dazedly. "When's Matt coming back to Carson?"

"Who knows?" Sally's smile was toothpaste bright. "He's such a busy man, and he knows we all like visiting him in New York. It's always a treat to go to his home in Chappaqua. He has all the modern conveniences and a nice big yard full of maple trees. An ideal place for children, I've always thought."

"I see," Linda said. "He isn't planning to come back for Jennifer and Doug's engagement party?"

"Shh!" Sally looked around nervously. "Greta Wittmeyer's at the end of the street, and I swear that woman has bionic ears."

"Sorry. But Matt won't be coming to the party?" Linda persisted.

"I don't expect so, dear. His schedule's horrendous with all the work he has to do for *American Eagle*. And, of course, there's no reason for him to come back, is there? I mean, you're quite right. He did behave badly to you, and I'm sure you'll never change your mind about marrying him. I mean, the two of you, you're not what I'd call an obvious combination. Nobody would consider a marriage between the pair of you sensible, and Lord knows, you're always sensible, right?"

"Right," Linda agreed miserably. "I'm always sensible."

Sally patted Linda's arm. "If you're feeling ready to date again, there are lots of nice local men. Greta Wittmeyer has a nephew who's a bank manager in Grand Junction. She's often mentioned what a wonderful couple you and he would make. I believe his hobby is insect collecting. Greta told me he has over a thousand mounted specimens."

"I despise insect collecting," Linda said tersely. "And I'm sure I'd loathe Greta Wittmeyer's nephew."

Sally's irritating good humor dropped away, like a cloak discarded as unnecessary. "You've sent Matt away twice, Lindy Beth. This time he won't come back unless you ask him." She turned and walked quickly down the garden path, leaving a frowning, speculative Linda staring after her.

Linda watched with wry amusement as the citizens of Carson went all out on the arduous task of transforming Matthew Deighton from official Black Sheep into the town's most famous Celebrity. The past was rewritten, his role in the Suzanne Mackenzie scandal explained, and his brilliance as an artist ascribed to the excellence of the courses at the local high school. The Grand Junction newspaper even printed an article proving that the inspiration for Grant Deighton's prize-winning sets all came from the towering majesty of the Rocky Mountains.

Sally Deighton, with a daughter on TV, a youngest son who was a pilot in the air force, and an eldest son who was a millionaire, suddenly found herself elevated to the proud position of Carson's Mother of the Year. She and Frank both found her rapid promotion highly amusing.

Carson's next self-imposed obligation was to choose

Matt a wife suited to his fame and fortune. Even without the fascinating stories of love and passion being spread by Greta Wittmeyer, the choice was obvious. The town's most famous native son deserved nothing less than the town's resident angel. Linda Petrie and Matthew Deighton. Even the names went well together. Carson—indifferent to minor facts like Matt's departure for New York and Linda's obstinate insistence that she had no idea when he would return—amused itself by planning the wedding. The general opinion was that the bride should wear pale blush pink and carry white orchids.

Linda began to dread her trips into town. Her progress along the street was invariably interrupted by one well-wisher after another inquiring about her upcoming wedding. The more fervently she insisted that she and Matt had no plans to marry, the more knowing the smiles of the townsfolk became.

By Wednesday morning, her nerves were shredded. She knew she couldn't blame the community for her lacerated temper and permanent headache. The only reason their gossip was driving her crazy was because it wasn't true. She left the twins in the backyard, squirting each other with water, and marched into the kitchen.

"Mom, could you keep an eye on Kate and Drew while I run something up on the sewing machine?"

Nora looked up from the ironing board. "You planning to sew something special?"

"A Rumble." Linda opened the fridge door and became very preoccupied with selecting a container of yogurt. She spoke without turning around. "I want to send it to Matt."

The silence in the kitchen stretched out for several seconds. "I'll keep an eye on the children," Nora said.

"We'll feed the ducks in the park, and then I'll drive into Grand Junction and give them lunch at McDonalds." Nora unplugged the iron. "That'll give you the whole morning to yourself."

"McDonalds!" Linda was startled enough to jerk her head out from behind the protection of the refrigerator door. "You're actually going to let your grandchildren eat fast food?"

"I guess a few greasy french fries won't ruin them for life."

Linda closed the fridge door, deciding she wasn't hungry enough to eat yogurt. "You've changed these past few days, Mom. What's happened?"

"Your father's thinking of retiring," Nora replied obliquely. "We thought we might buy a camper and see something of the country while we're still sufficiently young and healthy to enjoy touring. We've never visited the East Coast. Never been east of Chicago, in fact. Maybe it's past time for us to make a change."

"I see. Is New York on your itinerary, by any chance?"

"Could be. I've heard tell as how New England's real pretty in the fall."

"Mom, I don't know if Matt will come back, even if I ask him. He may not be interested in me anymore."

"Course he's interested. He's not a fool." Nora folded the ironing board and put it away in the cupboard. "I'll get the twins in from the yard, and I guess you'd better start work on that Rumble, although what you're going to do with it, I can't imagine. Maybe it's better if I don't try to imagine," she added darkly.

Linda finished sewing the Rumble at noon. It was a female Rumble, with demure, stubby arms clasped over its pot belly, and an expression of cross-eyed rapture that would have guaranteed the creature being banned from all respectable toy shops. Sewn onto its paw was a miniature postcard that read: *I love you. I miss you. Please come home soon.*

When the twins returned from their outing, they were more than willing to miss their afternoon nap and drive back into town so that Linda could take the package to the post office for express mailing to New York.

"Who is this present for?" Drew asked.

"It's for Matt."

"Is it Matt's birfday?" Kate wanted to know. In her limited experience, packages were synonymous with Christmas and birthdays.

"No, I just wanted to send him a message."

"When is he going to be our new daddy?" Drew asked, his voice entirely matter-of-fact, as if the subject had already been discussed at boring length and everything settled save the most trivial details.

Linda gulped, then turned to stare at her son. "Drew, it's not decided yet. Matt and I may not get married."

"You don't have to get married," Kate offered generously. "We just want Matt for our daddy. Drew and me like Matt. He smells good."

"Like ice cream," Drew supplied. After a moment's thought, he added, "Not so good as ice cream."

Linda laughed, although tears felt perilously close. "I'll see what I can do. Okay?"

"Okay." Kate craned her neck around to look out of the rear window. "I saw a deer," she said. "Did you see the deer, Mommy?"

"It wasn't a deer," Drew said scornfully.

"It was so. I'm biggerer than you and I saw it."

As far as the twins were concerned, the subject of Matt was obviously forgotten.

* * *

If Sally Deighton hadn't already achieved the pinnacle of local success, her party celebrating Jennifer's engagement to Doug would certainly have rocketed her straight to the top of Carson's social scene. The backyard was ablaze with late-summer flowers; the weather cooperated by being sunny, but not quite as hot as usual; and the food was wonderful.

Frank and Doug had spent a highly enjoyable morning constructing an oversize barbecue, and by midafternoon an assortment of potatoes, steaks, and hot dogs was sizzling over the coals. As if to prove that she could cook with the best of them when she cared to, Sally had prepared a dazzling array of salads and home-baked breads. Even Greta Wittmeyer could find nothing to complain about, a situation that threatened to ruin her enjoyment of the party.

Linda thought she might possibly be the only person in Carson who wasn't blissfully happy. Matt hadn't called. He wasn't at the party, and the Deightons didn't seem to be expecting him. Linda stared at the mustard congealing around her hot dog and wondered if anybody would notice if she left the party.

"Hi, Linda!" Becky Weaver bounced up before Linda could leave. "You're looking fabulous! You changed your hairstyle or something?"

"No, I just left it loose. This is a new outfit, though."

Becky squinted against the sun. "That's what it is! You're wearing red. I've never seen you in a bright color before." She chuckled. "Greta will be telling everybody you've turned into a scarlet woman. Where's Matt, by the way?"

Linda gritted her teeth. "I don't know," she said for about the twentieth time in the past hour. "I haven't heard from him."

Jennifer, looking radiant, came up with Drew and Kate in tow. "They were eating chocolate sprinkles straight out of the bowl," she explained to Linda. "You might want to sit with them in a quiet spot until their digestive systems go out of overload."

"Have you and Doug decided when you'll be getting married?" Becky asked as they all walked to a group of vacant chairs set in the shade.

"Not yet." Jennifer laughed. "The only thing we decided was that Kate should be the flower girl and Drew the ring bearer."

"Oh, so you're having a traditional ceremony?"

Jennifer actually blushed. "We both thought we would like that. Weddings are sort of traditional things when you get right down to it."

"I'm gonna be sick," Kate announced.

"Not here," Linda said quickly. "We'll find the bathroom."

"There's Matt," Drew said. "Hi, Matt! Kate's gonna be sick."

Linda rose to her feet. Matt halted a foot away from her. They stared silently into each other's eyes.

Kate tugged at Matt's dress slacks. "Hi, Matt. I'm gonna be sick."

Jennifer and Becky simultaneously grabbed for a twin's hand. "We'll be in the downstairs bathroom if you need us," Jennifer said.

Neither Linda nor Matt replied. Jennifer and Becky exchanged glances. Jennifer winked. "I'll catch you later, big brother."

"Yeah, good to see you, Matt." Becky propelled Kate toward the house, leaving Matthew and Linda alone together.

"Hi," Matt said.

Linda tried to sound casual. "Hi."

"The flight was late or I'd have been here sooner."

"I'm glad you're here now. I—missed you."

Matt held out a big white box tied with red ribbon. "I brought you a present."

All around them, the party ebbed and flowed. Linda was aware of nothing except the sound of her own heartbeat and Matt's nearness. "Should I open it now?"

"Please."

She pulled at the giant bow and lifted the lid from the box. Nestled on a bed of tissue paper, a pair of Rumbles lay clasped in each other's arms. The female Rumble was the one Linda had sent to Matt. The male Rumble was one she had never seen before. It stared up at her, its blue eyes distinctly pleading. For such an arrogantly male creature, its expression seemed endearingly hesitant. Attached to its paw was a miniature postcard. The card read: *I love you. I want you. Will you please marry me?*

Slowly, she lifted the male Rumble out of his bed. Pinned to the center of his sagging belly was a diamond engagement ring. She looked up at Matt, then unfastened the ring and held it out to him. "Will you put it on for me?"

"Does that mean yes?"

"It sure does."

He slipped the ring onto her finger, then pulled her into his arms and kissed her as if his life depended on it. She pressed herself to him, reveling in the unyielding hardness of his muscle against the softness of her body, savoring the completeness that she had never felt with anyone except Matt.

"I take it you're planning to announce the wedding date some time soon?"

Mrs. Wittmeyer's honeyed voice brought Linda back to earth with a bang. She felt the shudder of Matt's body against hers; then he slowly drew away his mouth, although he kept his arms firmly around her. When her eyes were at last capable of focusing on something other than Matt, she realized that the pair of them were surrounded by a small circle of fascinated townsfolk.

It was Sally Deighton who answered Greta Wittmeyer's question. "Matt and Linda are getting married at the same time as Jennifer and Doug. We're planning a double wedding for the last weekend in August."

Matt gave his mother a small grin. "We are?"

"We are," she repeated firmly. "Nora and I agreed on the date yesterday. Don't worry, Matt. Everything's taken care of."

Doug laughed and clapped Matt on the shoulder. "Here's some friendly advice from a man who's already been engaged for a whole week. Don't try to alter any arrangements. The wedding juggernaut is already rolling, and neither of us puny males is strong enough to stop it. It took me about three-and-a-half minutes to figure out that the groom's role in these proceedings is simply to nod his head yes whenever his prospective mother-in-law makes a suggestion."

"That doesn't sound too difficult. I think I should soon get the hang of it." Matt gave the assembled group of people a charming smile. "Talk to you all again later. Right now, Linda and I have to go round up the twins."

They dodged congratulations all the way up to the house. As soon as they were inside, Matt propelled her into the den and shut the door. He pulled her into his arms and pressed a row of urgent kisses along her neck and shoulder, imprinting her skin with the mark of his lips, and burning her soul with the heat of his desire.

"I love you, Matt," Linda said, when they finally stopped kissing long enough to speak. "These last few days, I've missed you so much I felt less than half-alive."

"I love you, too. When I went back to New York, my house seemed so empty I was scared. Ms. Rumble arrived in the nick of time to save my sanity."

She smiled. "Who made Mr. Rumble for you?"

"He's one of the first prototypes from Playbrite. I very nearly had to pledge my life savings to get Charlie to part with him." Matt cradled her hips with his hands and nuzzled her neck. "Any chance of persuading you upstairs to my bedroom some time in the near future?"

"Well, I don't know..." Linda pretended to consider, although her heart already raced with pleasurable anticipation. "I think I could clear a space in my calendar some time in the next five minutes."

"Let's go—"

The den door flew open with a bang. "I didn't be sick," Kate announced proudly. She walked into the room, followed by Drew. The twins looked intently at Linda and Matt, who were still locked in each other's arms.

"Are you my new daddy now?" Drew asked.

Matt broke off the embrace but still retained Linda's hand. He bent down so that he was at eye level with Drew. "I'm not your dad yet, but I will be soon. And then you'll be my son and Katie will be my daughter. We'll be a family. I'm looking forward to that."

Kate nodded. "We're going to live in your house. Granny says it'll have a swing set in the backyard. You want to see my new pink sneakers?"

"They're yellow," Drew corrected.

"They're pink," Kate insisted. "I'm bigger than you, so I know."

Drew looked from Matt to his sister and breathed

deeply. "You're not bigger than me, Katie, we're the same size. And they're *yellow* sneakers."

"All right, they're yellow." Kate gave her brother a sunny smile and patted her hair. "Want to see my yellow sneakers, Matt?"

"That would be great."

Linda and Matt straightened. Over the children's heads, their eyes met. Linda sighed. "August twenty-ninth. The honeymoon suite at the hotel of your choice. I'll bring a black lace negligee. Hold that thought."

Matt reached into his pocket and dangled a key enticingly in front of her. "Tonight, nine-thirty. The Hilton in Grand Junction. Forget the negligee. Hold that thought."

She smiled and pressed her fingers to his lips. "I'm holding."